# Readers Love Andrew Grey

## *An Isolated Range*

"Mr. Grey delivers a highly emotional story that captures the reader's heart in one fell swoop. This is an author who is dedicated to his series, stories and characters. With each range story, you always find yourself drawn in, breathless until the very last page is read."

—Dawn's Reading Nook

"Andrew Grey's Range series just gets stronger with each new book and *An Isolated Range* is perhaps the most amazing addition yet."

—Scattered Thoughts and Rogue Words

"*An Isolated Range* is a story not of human triumphs but also of sadness and death. This is an author who balances both so well that the reader is left speechless after that last page is read."

—Love Romances and More

## *The Fight Within*

"I loved this book, these characters, and this story. Get it today. Read. Understand and through understanding, enjoy."

—Mrs. Condit & Friends Read Books

"This is a story that is rich in detail, delving into the Native American culture and also sharing the suffering that the Native American's still face today."

—MM Good Book Reviews

"This was a very powerful read."

—Live your Life, Buy the Book

Novels by ANDREW GREY

Accompanied by a Waltz
Dutch Treat
A Heart Without Borders
In Search of a Story
Stranded
A Wild Ride • A Daring Ride
Three Fates (anthology)
Work Me Out (anthology)

ART SERIES
Legal Artistry • Artistic Appeal • Artistic Pursuits • Legal Tender

BOTTLED UP STORIES
Bottled Up • Uncorked • The Best Revenge • An Unexpected Vintage

CHILDREN OF BACCHUS STORIES
Children of Bacchus • Thursday's Child • Child of Joy

GOOD FIGHT SERIES
The Good Fight • The Fight Within • The Fight for Identity

LOVE MEANS… SERIES
Love Means… No Shame • Love Means… Courage • Love Means… No Boundaries
Love Means… Freedom • Love Means … No Fear
Love Means… Family • Love Means… Renewal • Love Means… No Limits

SENSES STORIES
Love Comes Silently • Love Comes in Darkness

SEVEN DAYS STORIES
Seven Days • Unconditional Love

STORIES FROM THE RANGE
A Shared Range • A Troubled Range • An Unsettled Range
A Foreign Range • An Isolated Range• A Volatile Range

TASTE OF LOVE STORIES
A Taste of Love • A Serving of Love • A Helping of Love • A Slice of Love

Published by DREAMSPINNER PRESS
http://www.dreamspinnerpress.com

Novellas by ANDREW GREY

A Present in Swaddling Clothes
Organic Chemistry
Shared Revelations
Snowbound in Nowhere
Whipped Cream

FIRE SERIES
Redemption by Fire • Strengthened by Fire • Burnished by Fire • Heat Under Fire

CHILDREN OF BACCHUS STORIES
Spring Reassurance • Winter Love

LOVE MEANS… SERIES
Love Means… Healing • Love Means… Renewal

WORK OUT SERIES
Spot Me • Pump Me Up • Core Training • Crunch Time
Positive Resistance • Personal Training • Cardio Conditioning

Published by DREAMSPINNER PRESS
http://www.dreamspinnerpress.com

# A DARING RIDE

ANDREW GREY

Published by
Dreamspinner Press
5032 Capital Circle SW
Ste 2, PMB# 279
Tallahassee, FL 32305-7886
USA
http://www.dreamspinnerpress.com/



A Daring Ride


Cover Art by L.C. Chase
http://www.lcchase.com



ISBN: 978-1-62798-097-5
Digital ISBN: 978-1-62798-098-2

Printed in the United States of America
First Edition
September 2013

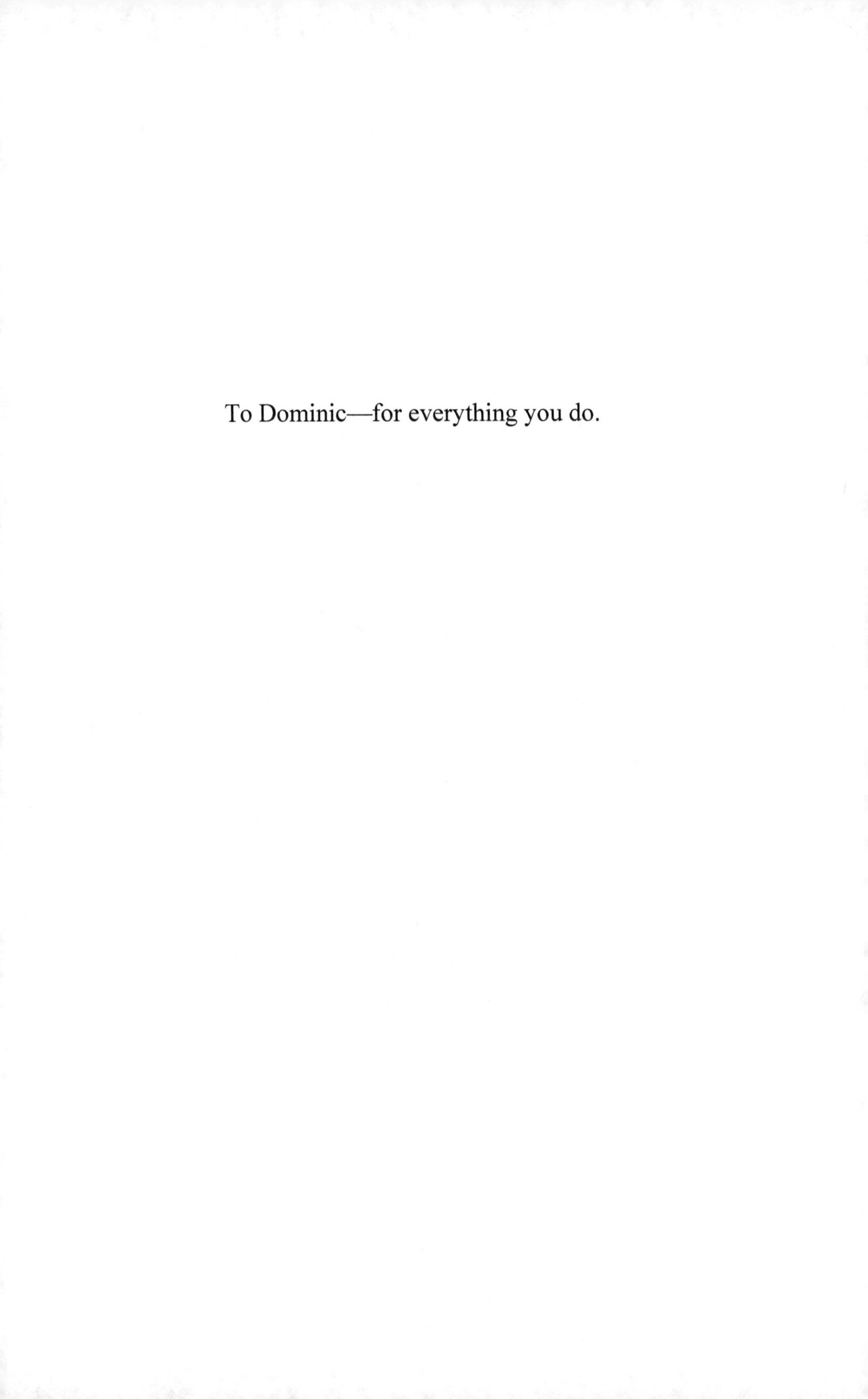

To Dominic—for everything you do.

# CHAPTER ONE

"HEY, kid, give 'em one hell of a show. That's all you need to do," said the old man standing near the bull chute as Simon Frizzell walked past to take his ride on Geronimo's Revenge, the bull he'd drawn. He kept the Frizzell part quiet and went by the nickname "Frizz," ostensibly because of his curly red hair. No one on the rodeo circuit knew his last name and everything that went along with it, and that was exactly how he wanted to keep it.

"I'll do my best," Simon said as he checked his equipment over for the last time and got into position. Bull rope, protective vest? Check. Hat, chaps? Check. Sanity? Well, by most people's standards that was debatable, but from the rush of blood through his body and the zing, bordering on a high, that sang through his brain, he could put a check behind that as well.

The handlers signaled that they were ready, and Simon climbed on the rail. "Ladies and gentlemen, Simon the Frizz will be riding Geronimo's Revenge, one of the meanest bulls on this part of the circuit. So put your hands together and let him hear it." *Simon the Frizz.* That was a new one, but he liked it. He heard the people in the stands around the outdoor ring whoop and holler. It was doubtful that any of them had ever heard of him before—this was only his sixth rodeo. He'd wanted to ride rodeo since he was big enough to sneak away from his folks' place to the ranch next door and pull himself up the fence so he could see the men practice busting broncs and take turns riding the bulls. This was what he'd always dreamed of doing.

Simon waved from the top of the fence, smiling wide and mugging for the crowd. Then he climbed over the fence and settled on the bundle of caged power that was Geronimo's Revenge. He could smell sweat and pure testosterone coming off the beast. He waved to the crowd one more time and then took hold of the rope, making sure his legs were in the proper position before giving the signal.

The bull leaped out of the gate, landed, and then bucked straight up, turning in midair, landing and then turning the other way. By sheer luck and the grace of God, Simon managed to stay on. He jumped again and began to whirl. Simon moved with him, trying his best to anticipate the animal's next move. His training said one thing, but that voice in his head told him something different. He went with the voice, and dad-gum, he was right. That fucking bull switched directions, but Simon was ready. It wasn't pretty, and he forgot to use his hand the way the professionals did to make it look easy, but he was still on. Simon yelled at the top of his lungs, shouting the joy of lasting this long to the universe. The bull switched gears again, and Simon felt his balance begin to go. *Just one more second.* He held on, using his legs to last just a split second more.

The bell sounded, and Geronimo's Revenge seemed to have had enough. He jumped straight up once again, then landed on his front hooves. His rear hooves touched the ground and then bounced right back up. Like being flung from a slingshot, Simon flew off his back. Thankfully, he had the presence of mind to let go of the rope, and instantly he was in the air, sailing over the bull. Simon landed and rolled, hoping like hell the bull didn't come after him. He'd only just come to a stop before he scrambled to his feet and raced toward the fence. He didn't even look back as he climbed the fence. Bang!

The fence shook, and Simon leaped over and onto the ground. He found his feet, barely, and one of the spectators grabbed his arm to keep him from sprawling into the stands.

"Whooee, what a ride!" the announcer called. "The kid's okay. Let's give him a hand for making the count!" The crowd cheered, and Simon went to take off his hat, but realized it was gone. Someone shoved it into his hand, and Simon turned in time to see one of the rodeo clowns nod to him. Simon waved the hat in return and then climbed on the fence, holding his hat high to the Saturday rodeo crowd while he waited for the score. "Well, folks, it wasn't pretty," the announcer said, and a chuckle went up from the ring of bleachers that lined the ring. "But Frizz stayed on Geronimo's Revenge, and that's a feat, I must say. The score for that ride is 87.3. He's in the money, folks." The crowd cheered once again.

Simon knew that because of his ranking, most of the score had been for the bull, but he'd take it. Like the announcer had said, it might not have been pretty, but he'd done it. Simon waved one last time and then climbed down from the fence and headed around the arena walkway toward the space between sets of bleachers.

"Frizz, you did it," Gardner cried as soon as Simon made his way behind the crowd. Simon and the bronc rider had formed a deep friendship over the years. They'd grown up relatively close together outside Oklahoma City and had discovered a mutual love of rodeo. Simon and Billy Bob—which was why he went by Gardner—shared rooms at rodeos to save expenses. Gardner's dad was like a second father to him, and they were the only two people who knew Simon's little secret. "Can't believe you stayed on that sumbitch!" Gardner teased.

"I can't either," a voice said from behind him, and Simon turned around. "You're either the luckiest bastard alive, or… damn, I don't know what else." The man was smiling, or else Simon would probably have taken a swipe at him. He'd just gone the distance; no one pissed on that.

"Dante, be nice," a good-looking man said from behind him. "He doesn't realize you're kidding." The other man turned to him. "Sorry. I'm Ryan, and this hellion is Dante Rivers. We watched your ride, and he said he wanted to congratulate you. If I'd known he was in one of his snarky moods, I'd have fed him first." Ryan shook his head and rolled his eyes while elbowing the other man in the ribs.

"You're Dante Rivers," Simon and Gardner said in near unison, and Simon swallowed hard. "It's good to meet you. I'm Simon, but the rodeo folks call me Frizz, and this is Gardner."

Dante smiled and shook his hand. "I was just teasing earlier, but you gotta admit you were lucky." Dante oophed when Ryan elbowed him again. "How did you stay on him after that spin and turn? How did you know to expect that move?"

"Don't know. Something in my head said what he was going to do. I thought I was nuts at the time, but I went with it," Simon answered.

Dante glanced at Ryan for a second, and they shared a brief look before turning back to him. "Well, that was a hell of a ride. And you deserve whatever you get for it. They said you're in the money, and not many guys are staying on today. It was nice to meet you, and regardless of my teasing earlier, congratulations. You did good." Dante smiled and turned to walk away.

"Sometimes you can be such an ass," Simon heard Ryan say as they moved away. The rest of their conversation was drowned out by the crowd.

"Well, that was pretty cool," Gardner said.

"Yeah, he said I did good, but only after in essence saying I was the luckiest guy out there today." The more he thought about it, the more he wondered why Dante had bothered to stop by at all.

"Hey, the guy he was with said he was kidding. Believe him and move on. You rode pretty well, and you're still learning. It looks like you'll finish in the money, and who knows? It's hard for me to tell, but I haven't heard a score higher than yours yet, so you may be in the lead and could win a buckle. Either way, you'll come out ahead, and that's never a bad thing." Gardner slapped him on the back, and Simon knew it was the truth. They shifted to a spot where they could watch the rest of the riders. Guys rode pretty well, some staying on and some getting bucked. One guy drew a bull that, when they opened the chute, walked out looking like it was going to lie down or look for flowers to smell. The cowboy kicked it, and it bucked a few times and then settled down again.

"Looks like my luck's holding," Simon said. This was a small rodeo without a large entrance fee or purse, but still, it would be nice to win something.

Finally, the last rider was up, and Simon held his breath and waited to see what happened. The bull jumped out and looked good; so did the cowboy. He was smooth, and damn if every movement wasn't fluid grace in motion. He hadn't heard the announcement as to who the rider was, but Simon was mesmerized. There was no excess movement, and the rider seemed to know what the bull was going to do even before the bull did. His body flowed with every move, hips and legs remaining perfectly positioned, his arm flowing back and forth. It was like this guy wrote the textbook for this bull. Where he'd come from and what he was doing at this rodeo was beyond Simon, but he watched and took in every second of that ride. When the bell sounded, the rider bailed, landed on his feet and hurried to the fence.

"That's what I want to be able to do. Ride like that and be able to play the bull like a fucking violin," Simon whispered. He didn't care if anyone heard because those words were meant for himself. That was what he'd wanted since he was seven years old.

"Ladies and gentlemen, that was a bit of a surprise for you. We had an extra spot, and that, my friends, was Texas's very own Dante Rivers, Professional Bull Riding World Champion. Let's give it up and thank him for giving us all a great show," the announcer said with amplified enthusiasm. The spectators came to their feet, whistling, stomping, and cheering, while Simon watched Dante wave his hat to the crowd.

Once everyone had settled down, the winners were announced, and Simon had come in second. Not that it really mattered. Sure, he'd have liked to have won, but he'd had his best rodeo ride ever on a pretty highly ranked bull. That was a success in his book. So he hurried into the center of the arena when his name was called, waved his hat, and acknowledged the applause as he accepted his prize.

He was still smiling when he left the arena and wove his way through the departing crowd and into the rider's ready area to get his equipment. He packed everything in his oversized duffel and slung it over his back.

"You going for a drink?" Gardner asked as he joined him, carrying his own bag.

"I was thinking about it," Simon said with a smile and followed his friend out to where Simon's truck was parked. They threw their bags in the back and climbed inside. He started the engine and turned on the AC before getting in line to leave the rodeo grounds and head to the local watering hole.

When they pulled in, the place was already packed, and Simon had a hard time finding a spot to park. He managed to snag the last one at the end of the last row. After parking, they walked toward the bar. "Feels like I've got half the arena sand in my throat," Simon said as he lifted his hat and ran his fingers through his wild red hair, futilely trying to tame it. Then he gave up and plopped his hat back down. Maybe he should just cut the shit off.

"Come on, pretty boy," Gardner teased. "Let's go have some fun."

"Look who's talking," Simon said, lightly pushing Gardner, who easily bumped him back. Simon yanked open the door to the bar, and they walked inside. The place was old and like a million other watering holes on the edge of small towns in rodeo country—rough interior that had seen multiple bar fights, with tables and chairs that could be easily replaced. The best part about the place was the back bar, which someone had obviously taken great care to craft. It was definitely something out of the previous century, and Simon figured the bar had to have been built around it.

"Find us a table, and I'll get some beer," Gardner said, and Simon nodded, then wove through the crowd in a futile attempt to find an empty table. Hell, there was barely an empty spot of floor in the place, let alone anywhere to sit.

"Frizz," he heard someone say as he reached one end of the room. "Frizz." He turned around and saw someone wave. It took him a second to realize it was Ryan, the guy with Dante Rivers. He waved again, and Simon headed over toward him. "Wanna join us?" Ryan asked. "Dante braved the crowd around the bar for something to drink."

"Thanks. Gardner's doing the same," Simon said and approached the table. Another man was sitting with Ryan, and Simon pulled out the chair across from him.

"This is a good friend of ours, Jacky," Ryan said, and they shook hands. "He's traveling with us. Sometimes it seems like he lives with us, but he has his own place in Houston," Ryan teased, and Jacky smiled at him a little more widely than Simon would have expected. Simon nodded in acknowledgement, doing his best not to ogle the lithe man, probably in his late twenties, who crackled with energy. Then he turned to try to see Gardner, but the people were three thick around the bar and he couldn't find him. Eventually he spotted him, and Simon excused himself and hurried to where Gardner was fighting the crowd for a place.

"We have a table over there with Dante Rivers," Simon said excitedly, and Gardner narrowed his eyes slightly. "What?"

"Are you sure that's a good idea?"

"I already sat down. Why?" Simon asked.

"That guy Ryan, you know he's not just the guy's friend. There was a bit of a ruckus a few years ago when Dante"—Gardner leaned closer—"came out of the closet, if you know what I mean." Gardner tilted his head slightly, and Simon felt the fluttery buzz of a million bees working in his stomach. He knew that feeling well, the mixture of fear and excitement whenever he thought he might be around guys who liked guys. He'd felt it a number of times, but there was no way he could have done anything about it. Now he might have a chance. "You know your folks would have a fit if they knew you were riding rodeo, but they'd come unglued and explode if they even just thought you were hanging with people like that."

"What are you, my conscience? Look at this place. It's jammed, and they invited us to join them. Dante's a famous bull rider, a world champion. What if it was Harvey Marks and you had the chance to ask questions of the bronc-busting great? Would you turn it down?" Simon hoped he didn't sound too excited or anxious in his argument. "No, you wouldn't. And they invited us."

"But what if…."

"What? They start cruising you or something?" Simon cracked in what he hoped was disarming humor, but it hit just a little closer to home than he'd wanted. Jacky had been watching him with his deep-blue eyes ever since Simon got up from the table—he could almost feel his gaze on him now.

Gardner laughed, and Simon laughed with him. "I'll get the beer and join you over there," Gardner said and managed to take a step closer to the bar. Simon got out of the way and wove back through the crowd toward the table. Dante had returned, and Simon sat down where he'd been. Dante had gotten extra beers, and he offered one to Simon.

"I wasn't about to brave that crush again for more," he said as explanation for the extra glasses on the table. "Those boys are nuts today."

Simon gulped from the glass, peering over it at Jacky. He tried not to smile, but failed, and he saw Jacky notice. Simon's heart raced faster, and he did his best not to choke on his beer. He lowered

the glass and set it on the table, then turned away, ostensibly to look for Gardner, but it was suddenly getting warm in there.

Gardner set more glasses on the table and sat down next to him. Brief introductions were made. “Do you ride bulls too?” Jacky asked Gardner.

“No, he rides broncs,” Simon said, and then he quickly gulped from his glass to keep the naughty thoughts running through his mind from showing on his face.

“I tried that a few times when I was a kid, but I wasn’t as in tune with the horses,” Dante said and then turned to Simon. “You had a couple of good rides today. You’ve got talent, that’s for sure.” Dante then lifted his glass and looked toward Ryan. Simon followed his gaze and was glad he wasn’t taking a drink at that moment. The heat and electricity between Dante and Ryan was impossible to miss. Simon glanced around, but no one else seemed to see it. Well, with the exception of Jacky, who definitely seemed to see what Simon did.

Simon set his glass on the table and let go of it, his hands shaking. All his life he’d been told in sneaky, roundabout ways, clothed in holier-than-thou speech, that what he felt was wrong. And yet here were Dante and Ryan, each looking like the other man hung the moon.

“Hi,” one of the rodeo bunnies said as she came over to the table. She plopped right down on Gardner’s lap, and Simon nearly fell off his chair.

“Well, how are you, honey?” Gardner asked, handing her a beer without missing a beat. She giggled and wiggled her chest in Gardner’s face.

“I saw you ride today and thought you were amazing,” she said. Simon turned away and tried not to make some crack. Out of the corner of his eye, he saw her lean in and whisper something in Gardner’s ear. She giggled again, and Gardner pulled her a little closer. Obviously their hotel room was going to see some action, and it looked like Simon would have to wait out in the cold. That wasn't unusual. Gardner wasn't particularly handsome, not in the conventional sense, but women flocked to him. Simon had never really figured it out, but the guy could walk into a bar, smile at a girl, and she'd come over to talk and end up going home with Gardner. That's just the way it was. Maybe it was the way he could purse his lips just so, and every girl wanted to kiss the hurt away. But Simon really thought it was his smile. It lit a room, and everyone, man or woman, wanted to bask in the glow. Either way, he was on tonight, and the buxom brunette sure seemed to have been caught in his gravity.

"Honey, I think you're pretty amazing," Gardner told her a bit predictably, but she smiled and leaned close again, whispering. Gardner stiffened, and then he whispered something back and the woman giggled once again. Simon finished his beer and looked at the others.

"Have you been riding bulls for a long time?" Jacky asked.

"Jacky's a real rodeo fan. He's been following the sport for years," Ryan said.

"You haven't?" Simon asked Ryan, wondering just how he and Dante met if Ryan wasn't a rodeo follower.

"Not until I met Dante. Jacky's the real fan, and he dragged me to the rodeo where I first saw Dante. He also dragged me to the bar afterwards, where I got the chance to meet him. The rest, as they say, is history." Ryan smiled.

"It's quite a story," Jacky said, his blue eyes sparkling. "Looks like your friend has plans for the evening."

Simon watched as Gardner and the girl stood up. Gardner finished his beer and put the glass back on the table. "I'll see you gentlemen later," he said with a wink and then headed toward the exit.

"Is he leaving you without a ride?" Jacky asked, and Simon shook his head.

"I learned a long time ago to make sure I had my own ride. So we take my truck. Gardner figures out his own way back, one way or another." He always had. Sometimes the nights were long when Simon got back and found their room occupied, but Gardner usually went to the girl's place.

"Well, that's good," Ryan said.

Simon nodded in agreement and drained the last of the beer from his glass. It also meant another night alone, but there wasn't much he could do about that. "Were you all in town for the rodeo?" Simon asked after setting down his glass. It wasn't a big enough attraction to pull people from very far. "I mean, it's a nice event and all."

"We've been on a bit of a road trip. Since Dante retired he's had some time on his hands, and I could tell he was getting a touch of the old wanderlust, so we were taking a vacation and saw the ads for the rodeo. Between Dante and Jacky, I was outnumbered," Ryan said with a chuckle. "Not that I'm really complaining." Ryan turned to Dante and his expression hardened. "I didn't know he was going to pull that little stunt with the bull this afternoon, though." Ryan stood up and stepped away from the table.

"Ryan, I was only having a little fun," Dante said before following, leaving Simon alone at the table with Jacky.

"Is he really mad that Dante rode?" Simon asked, following them through the crowd with his gaze.

"I think so, yeah. Dante didn't tell him he was going to do that, and then Ryan was nervous the entire time Dante was in the ring." Jacky shifted his gaze, and Simon followed it to where the two of them stood talking. Simon heard a small sigh from Jacky. "They're like each other's other half. Ryan stood by him, supported and encouraged him until he retired from riding bulls. He thought he was safe, but today scared him. Dante still wants to be able to ride even if he's getting older, and the thought scares Ryan to death."

"Isn't Dante over thirty?" Simon asked. That was ancient for a bull rider, at least as far as competition went. The sport was so hard on the body that not many lasted much longer.

"Yeah, but that doesn't mean he doesn't miss it or has lost the desire to ride," Jacky said.

"So Ryan wasn't really angry?"

Jacky shook his head. "Naw, just scared." They watched as Dante and Ryan wove back through the crowd toward the table. They weren't holding hands or even touching, but they might as well have been, the way they seemed to gravitate toward each other.

"Are you ready to go back to the hotel?" Dante asked Jacky, and then he glanced at Ryan.

"If you're not, I'll give you a ride," Simon offered before he could lose his nerve.

"If you're sure," Jacky said with a smile and then turned to Ryan and Dante. "I'll catch a ride with Frizz, and you two can get some rest." Jacky ducked Ryan's lighthearted swipe, and the two of them laughed.

"Call if you need anything," Ryan said, and then he and Dante headed toward the door.

"So, what did you have in mind?" Jacky asked just as Simon picked up another beer. Simon gulped and then swallowed hard as Jacky stared intently across the table. He lowered his glass, and even though he'd just been drinking, Simon's throat went dry. He swallowed once again and his eyes widened. The automatic denial of his desires was on the tip of his tongue, but he couldn't do it. This was the chance he'd wished for, dreamed of at night, ever since he could remember.

"How did you know?" Simon asked, and Jacky smiled as he leaned over the table.

"I didn't until just a few seconds ago. But I thought you were handsome and I was hoping that maybe we could spend some time together." Jacky smiled. "I've loved rodeo for years, and I always wanted the chance to be with a real cowboy." Jacky stood up, and Simon could almost see he was shaking with excitement.

He finished his beer in a few gulps for courage and then walked toward the door. Jacky came a few seconds behind him and followed Simon to his truck.

"This is really nice," Jacky said as he climbed inside. "I expected something older. Aren't most rodeo cowboys hard up for money?"

Simon walked around to the driver's side and got in, then started the engine and carefully pulled out of the parking lot. "Is your hotel in town?" Simon asked, ignoring the other man's question as he gripped the wheel tighter. He was so nervous he could hardly stand it.

"Yes. We're staying at the Saddle Post," Jacky said, and Simon nodded. He'd seen it on the way in, and since the town wasn't that big, it should be easy enough to find it again. "Have you done anything like this before?" Jacky asked, and Simon stared out the front window and slowly shook his head. "Never?"

"No. My family… they're…." He nearly told Jacky about them but clammed up. "They're protective. They don't even know I'm here. They think I went to a Bible retreat with some friends. My folks would flip out if they knew I was riding rodeo." *Let alone in a truck with another man planning to go back to his hotel room.* Simon kept that part quiet. Jacky didn't need to know all the details of his life, and Simon wasn't about to go into it. He'd learned that with too much information, people caught on quickly.

"How old are you?" Jacky asked softly.

That made Simon chuckle. "Twenty-two," he answered. "I'm not some sort of freak, am I?"

"No. That makes you a nice kid from what's most likely a small town. There's nothing wrong with you," Jacky told him reassuringly. "You know, we don't have to do anything. You can just drop me off at my hotel and go on back to yours. I don't want you to be uncomfortable."

"It isn't that. This is just something new." Simon swallowed hard as he made the turn at the edge of town. "What if I'm not any good?"

Jacky chuckled. "I bet you've probably been fantasizing about being with another guy since you were fourteen. I know I was."

Simon pulled into the hotel parking lot, and Jacky directed him to one of the rooms. Simon parked and turned off the engine, staring out the window at the door to the room. His stomach was turning flips, and he alternated between fear and excitement. Jacky was a good-looking man, and Simon had been thinking about being with someone for so long. He could hardly believe he was here now with another guy. Simon opened his door and got out. Jacky did the same. The doors thunked closed behind them, and Simon waited while Jacky unlocked the room door, then followed him inside.

Jacky turned on a light. The room wasn't much, but it was a bit bigger than the one Simon had with Gardner, and it was clean. "Take a seat," Jacky said, and then he walked through the room to the bathroom and closed the door. Simon looked around the room, not letting his eyes linger on the bed for too long. Maybe this wasn't such a good idea. Jacky seemed like a nice guy, but maybe Simon should just say good-bye when he came back out and go on back to his hotel. He shifted on the chair and was about to stand up to leave when Jacky came out of the bathroom. Simon had half expected him to come out naked or in his underwear, but Jacky was still dressed. He took off his light jacket and threw it over the back of a chair.

"Are you really okay?" Jacky asked.

"Yeah," Simon answered without moving.

"Like I said, we don't have to do anything," Jacky reiterated. He walked over and pulled out the other chair and sat down. "How long have you been riding rodeo?"

"I used to sneak away when I was a kid to the neighboring ranch and watch the men practice. I wanted to try, but my mom and dad would have none of it. As a teenager, I learned to ride, to my mother's consternation, but that was all I could ever push her to give permission for. When my mom was a girl, her brother was killed. Mom would never say how, but when I was old enough I started doing research on the Internet and at the library and found out he was killed riding bulls. He was thrown and apparently trampled to death. Mom never talks about it."

"So your folks have no idea at all?"

Simon shook his head. "I keep all my stuff at Gardner's and don't talk about it. My dad might suspect, but he doesn't really know, and he won't say anything to Mom. He doesn't really care that much and he's way too busy. But they'd both really care about me doing this." Simon sighed.

"You know, sometimes you have to do what makes you happy rather than what everyone else thinks you should do," Jacky said. "God, that sounded pompous. I didn't mean to." Jacky stood up and slowly stepped closer to where Simon waited nervously. Jacky leaned in, and Simon held his breath. Then Jacky kissed him, softly and gently.

Simon wasn't quite sure what to do at first. "Was that okay?" Simon asked when Jacky pulled away. Jacky smiled and leaned in again. This time, Simon kissed him back. Jacky seemed to like it, because he moaned softly and then kissed him harder. Simon felt Jacky's tongue on his lips and he opened his mouth. Jacky continued kissing him, traced the outline of his mouth, and then lightly sucked on his lower lip. Simon groaned and then cut the sound off. Jacky broke the kiss and chuckled, warm air flowing over Simon's skin. Jacky straightened back up and extended his hand. Simon took it and let Jacky pull him to his feet.

It seemed funny to him. Simon wasn't a big man—bull riders weren't generally very large—but Jacky was a bit smaller and yet Simon easily let him take control. That idea rankled, and as they got close to the bed, Simon pounced. They tumbled onto the mattress, Jacky laughing as they clung together. They rolled a bit until Simon ended up on top of Jacky, straddling his body. He smiled down at the other man and then leaned in to kiss him. Jacky wrapped his arms around Simon's neck and pulled him closer, deepening the kiss until they were both whimpering.

Simon ground his hips into Jacky's, and in the confines of his jeans, his dick throbbed. Jacky pulled Simon's shirt from his pants, and Simon gasped and his breath hitched as Jacky slipped his hands under Simon's shirt and stroked his skin. Without thinking, he closed his eyes and held still. Being touched like this by another man made Simon's head throb. His excitement was almost overwhelming.

"Breathe," Jacky cooed softly. "Just breathe and relax." Jacky kissed him again and then slowly rolled them on the bed. Now it was Simon's turn to be pressed into the mattress, and he loved it, loved Jacky's weight on him. Jacky smiled a wicked smile and then went to work on Simon's shirt. Once he got the buttons open, Jacky parted the fabric and splayed his hands against Simon's chest. "Damn," Jacky breathed as he ran his hands over Simon's skin, leaving a trail of heat wherever he touched.

"You're magic," Simon whispered. Jacky leaned forward and licked Simon's skin. Simon gasped as a zing of heat shot through him. Jacky chuckled and then brought his lips to one of Simon's nipples, lightly sucking and then licking the sensitive skin. Simon moaned even louder and thrust his chest forward in a silent plea for more. Jacky sucked harder, swirling his tongue and driving Simon nearly out of his mind with the new sensation of warmth and passion.

Then, all sensation stopped. Simon opened his eyes and sat up as Jacky pulled his shirt over his head, displaying a pale, surprisingly sculpted chest. He stretched long with his arms over his head. "I like your muscles," Simon whispered.

"I go to the gym as much as I can," Jacky said as he tossed his shirt aside.

Simon wrapped his arms around Jacky's waist and tugged him close, kissing him and then slowly licking his warm skin, where he got a hint of salt and sweat tinged with a touch of sweetness. Simon had no one to compare the flavor with, but he imagined that combination to be a flavor unique to Jacky. At least he hoped it was.

Jacky arched his back, and Simon continued licking and tasting. Simon tugged open Jacky's belt and pulled it off, then dropped it to the floor before running his fingers just inside the waistband of Jacky's pants. Simon wasn't sure what he was supposed to do, but he knew what he liked, so he tugged open Jacky's jeans. Jacky sighed and then squirmed away. Simon wondered what he'd done wrong for a few seconds until Jacky pressed him back on the mattress. Then Jacky pushed his pants down his legs and stepped out of them.

Simon's mouth went dry as Jacky, naked, climbed back on the bed. Simon's gaze involuntarily went to Jacky's full cock, slowly rocking back and forth with each step. As Jacky joined him on the bed, Simon reached out and ran his palm along its length. He knew his cock well, but feeling another's was a completely different sensation.

"You feel so good," Jacky whispered, and Simon curled his hand around Jacky's length as Jacky pulled open Simon's jeans and belt. Simon gasped when Jacky pushed down his boxers and took him firmly in his hand. Simon had touched himself many times, but it was nothing like having someone else touch him. He bucked lightly and Jacky agreeably tightened his grip. Simon thrust his hips forward, and Jacky smiled and lightly stroked him. Simon did the same and wondered at the blissful expression that bloomed on Jacky's face.

Jacky released him and tugged down Simon's pants. Simon kicked off his boots, and soon he was lying on the bed naked. Jacky climbed on top of him, skin to skin. There had been many times in his life that Simon had dreamed of being with another man like this, feeling his skin, his warmth against him. He had begun to think it might never happen. Jacky kissed him, hard and deep, nearly stealing Simon's breath away. Simon thrust his hips, and he felt Jacky doing the same. His cock moved over warm, slick skin. He could barely control himself. Jacky continued kissing him as they moved together. It didn't take long for Simon's thrusts to become ragged, and he heard Jacky's breathing shift and become more shallow. Simon was right on the edge. He clamped his eyes closed and his breath caught as he tumbled over the edge and came between them.

Jacky followed closely behind, and then Simon wrapped his arms around Jacky's shoulders and closed his eyes as the other man lightly kissed him. "Wow," Simon whispered.

"You can say that again, cowboy," Jacky whispered back. "That was something." Jacky made no indication he was going to move, and Simon liked it that way. He'd heard stories, read books, stuff like that, of men who pulled what a woman in one of the stories called a "shoot and scoot." Simon was glad Jacky didn't seem to be like that. Simon had half expected to be asked to leave so Jacky could go to bed. Instead, Jacky got up after a while and went to the bathroom, then returned with a towel. He wiped them off quickly and then threw the towel in the corner before getting back in bed and turning out the light.

"I thought you'd want me to leave," Simon whispered. He had no experience with these kinds of things, but Jacky curled next him and rested his head on Simon's shoulder.

"Nope," Jacky said. "The way I figure it, you're young and you just had a taste of what you've wanted and dreamed about for a long time. So I figured I'd give you a chance to rest for a little while and then I'd see what other sorts of fun things we can get up to." Jacky stroked his chest, and Simon closed his eyes. "You're a really handsome man, and I like you," Jacky added.

"I like you too," Simon whispered. He wasn't really tired, but he was unbelievably relaxed and he liked that feeling. So much of his life consisted of watching what he said and trying to hide his true feelings and thoughts. That took more energy and diligence than he ever thought possible. For the first time he could remember, Simon didn't have to pretend with someone, at least not about the really important things. He snorted slightly. "Do you realize you know things about me my family doesn't? And they'd probably never speak to me if they did?"

Jacky stroked Simon's chest, bumping his fingers over Simon's nipples one at a time. "Everyone thinks that. It's one of the great fallacies of coming out. Your fear of how the people in your life will react is usually worse than the reality. I was so scared to tell my folks, but when I did, my mother asked me why I'd taken so long, and my father just rolled his eyes. They'd apparently known I was gay for years and neither of them gave a fig about it. They loved me anyway. And I think that's what most people experience. Sure, there are exceptions, mostly people exaggerating what happened in order to make a good story, but I think most parents truly love their children, and while they might be hurt at first, the love of their children takes over and that's what's really important."

"I wish that were true," Simon said. "In my case, I'm probably giving my folks the benefit of the doubt as to how upset they'll be." He shifted on the mattress and wished he hadn't brought up this particular subject. He hated to think about it, let alone talk about it. No matter what he did, Simon saw himself living some portion of a lie for quite a while. "Let's talk about something more fun, like you."

"I'm not that interesting," Jacky said, and Simon shivered when Jacky slowly ran his hand up his side. "I'm just a guy who really likes rodeo and loves the guys who have the guts and the balls to ride." Jacky shifted next to him and slowly began licking Simon's skin. Damn, that felt good, and Simon moaned softly. Jacky shifted and straddled Simon, rocking his hips back and forth. Within seconds, Simon was raring to go, and it looked like Jacky was right behind him. He wrapped a hand around Jacky's cock, stroking slowly while Jacky continued moving, running his tight little butt up and down Simon's length.

"Damn, you're something else," Simon said, and he cupped Jacky's butt, pressing his hips upward and his cock tighter to Jacky's skin.

"Ever wonder what it was like to be inside?" Jacky asked, and Simon shuddered with unfettered excitement. "I can tell you it's like nothing else you've ever felt in your life," Jacky said as he leaned forward, whispering in Simon's ear. "My body will grip you tight and not let go, and you'll feel like you sank into molten heat the likes of which you won't believe." Simon shook at the thought. "You'll fill me up like nothing else, and when you start to move, I'll tighten around you and your head will throb." Jacky sucked on his ear, and Simon held him closer, his cock jumping and throbbing between their bodies.

"Jacky," Simon whispered.

"And that isn't all," Jacky whispered, slowly shifting. He took Simon's hand and sucked on first one finger and then two, running his tongue around the digits. Simon could hardly believe what Jacky was doing to him. Granted, it was just words and finger sucking, but each movement was so sensual… his mind raced with all the possibilities.

As Jacky slowly slid down his body, Simon's fingers slipped from Jacky's lips, and Jacky gently kissed Simon's belly before continuing lower. When Simon felt Jacky's lips at the top of his hip, he held his breath, praying for what he hoped was coming next. "Damn," he groaned when Jacky slid his lips along the spine of his cock, moving up and down, slicking the skin. Then he pulled back and blew hot air over the wetness. Simon throbbed, his cock jumping with the cool heat.

"Was that good?" Jacky asked, and all Simon could do was moan and whimper for more. Jacky chuckled and then sucked the head of Simon's cock into his mouth.

Simon could hardly breathe. He'd fantasized about what this would feel like, but nothing could have prepared him for the real thing. His dick was surrounded by wet heat that pulled him deeper and deeper. Simon attempted to thrust forward impatiently, but Jacky stilled him with a hand on his hip and then sucked him deeper. "Jesus Christ!" Simon swore as he felt Jacky's nose press to his skin. "You're trying to kill me."

"Oh no, cowboy," Jacky said once he'd pulled away. "I'm not going to kill you, but I am going to send you to heaven." Jacky licked the very tip of his cock and then slowly slid his lips over the head and down the shaft. Simon had never experienced anything like this. He lightly combed his fingers through Jacky's soft hair as he bobbed his head. Simon resisted the urge to control the movement and went with it. Somehow he didn't think it would be good manners to ram himself down Jacky's throat. How he knew that he wasn't sure, but he let Jacky set the pace, and what a pace it was. Jacky bobbed his head, taking Simon deep and then backing away, only to take him deep again. Sometimes Jacky would hold him still, and Simon would feel his throat muscles working around him.

More than once he was so close to losing it, he could barely think. "Jacky," Simon cried, feeling Jacky swirl his tongue around the head of his cock. "I'm not going to last if you keep that up."

"Don't want you to," Jacky told him and did it again. Simon's cock throbbed and pulsed, with Simon just keeping himself from coming. Jacky looked up at him, eyes shining. "I want you to come so hard you forget your own name."

Simon chuckled quietly, wishing Jacky would get back to what he was doing.

"You don't think I can? Is that some sort of challenge?" Jacky asked, and before Simon could shake his head or tell Jacky no, his breath whooshed from his lungs as Jacky swallowed him whole. Hard and deep he sucked. Simon would not have been surprised if there had been no skin left on his dick once Jacky was through, and he didn't give a damn. Jacky sucked and swallowed, bobbing his head, faster and faster. The sensations rippled through Simon's body and mind, building on top of each other until they compounded again and again. Simon tried to take a breath, but kept failing as Jacky stole it over and over.

"Jacky!" Simon cried and gripped the bedding in his fists as his balls drew up close to his body and he tilted on the edge of the precipice of pleasure. Jacky held him there for second upon second before sucking him harder and driving Simon over the edge. He came in a blinding flash. He completely lost track of time, and Jacky was right—by the time he caught his breath, Simon didn't give a damn who or where he was. All he wanted was for the dreamy, floaty sensation to last forever.

Of course it didn't, and Simon came back to himself. He opened his eyes to find Jacky's shining back at him. Then Jacky kissed him. The flavor was different this time, and Simon realized it must have been from him. Simon deepened the kiss and rolled Jacky on the bed. He pressed him into the mattress and kissed him hard before licking down Jacky's neck and chest.

"You don't have to do that if you aren't ready," Jacky said.

"Is that a challenge?" Simon asked with a smile.

"No. It's just a fact. I don't want you to feel obligated to do anything. I know I made you happy, and it was incredibly erotic to watch you. That's all that's really necessary."

While Jacky went on, Simon kissed his way down Jacky's chest, licking his small pink nipples before continuing down his belly. Jacky's breath hitched, and Simon smiled before licking his way up Jacky's length. Instantly, Jacky's flavor, the one he'd gotten some of from licking his skin, burst on Simon's tongue. He licked again and then slowly slipped his lips over the head of Jacky's thick cock. The taste was intense, and Simon hummed around Jacky's cock. He carefully took more and more of Jacky in his mouth. He took too much and backed off quickly.

"It's okay," Jacky soothed. "Take it easy." He stroked Simon's hair and gently massaged his scalp.

Simon sucked deeper and then pulled back, moving his lips up and down Jacky's length. Then he used his hand and moved it along Jacky's length in time with his lips.

Jacky moaned and moved gently with him. Simon loved that he was making Jacky happy, and those sounds were like music to his ears. The small moans and whimpers filled the hotel room, encouraging Simon to work harder. He sucked and hummed around Jacky's cock, the first one other than his own he'd ever touched. And Simon had never imagined how exciting it would feel to have Jacky's thick cock gliding over his tongue again and again. He tried the swirly thing Jacky had done to him, and he must have done it right because Jacky whimpered softly.

"God, you're a natural," Jacky whimpered and then shook slightly. Simon took the encouragement to heart and increased his efforts, sucking harder. Almost instantly, Jacky's moaning became louder and he increased his thrusting. "So close," Jacky whispered and then pulled away. Jacky stroked himself, and within seconds Simon felt wet heat against his skin.

"Why'd you do that?" Simon asked once Jacky's moans had stopped.

"It isn't safe. I knew you hadn't been with anyone else, but I have been, and while I know I'm clean, I didn't want to put you at any risk," Jacky said, lightly tugging Simon back up toward him. Simon settled on the bed next to Jacky and hugged him close.

In some ways, this was the best part. They didn't talk, but Jacky held him. Simon's mind raced a mile a minute over what he'd just done and its full implications. Up to now, the thoughts and feelings he'd had were just that. Now they were real and had been turned into action. Simon lay on his side and stared at the curtains, thinking about what he'd just done and what he wanted.

It wasn't long before Jacky fell asleep. Simon checked the clock next to the bed and slowly got up. He used the light peeking in from between the curtains to find his clothes. He tugged them on as quietly as he could. In the movies this always seemed easy, but now, in the quiet room, every sound he made seemed as loud as a gunshot. He managed to dress and find all his stuff, strewn all over the floor. Then he leaned over the bed and watched Jacky sleep for a few seconds, wishing he could have more than just one night. But that was all they'd get. Silently, Simon turned and walked to the door. He opened it and took one final look at Jacky's nakedness resting on the bed. He suppressed the sigh that threatened and left the hotel room.

Simon walked to his truck and got inside. He closed the door as quietly as he could before remembering it didn't matter. Then he started the engine and backed out of the parking space before heading back to his hotel. He found a parking space not too far from the room. He wasn't sure what he'd be walking in on, so he went quietly. He half expected to see Gardner in bed with the girl he'd taken home from the bar, but when he unlocked the door, the beds were still made with their crisp corners and smooth bedspreads. Simon closed the door and sat on the edge of his bed, wondering what he was going to do. The genie was out of the bottle—he'd done things he'd enjoyed and wanted to do again. There was no way he could go back to being the same person he'd been just a few hours earlier, but he really didn't have a choice. He knew he had to lock away the amazing experience he'd just had… and all the feelings and longings that went with it.

He could still smell Jacky on his skin, and while he liked it, he couldn't stay that way. Simon went to the bathroom and took a quick shower, trying to be quiet for the people in the next room. Once he was done, Simon put his dirty clothes in his bag and laid out fresh ones for the morning, then pulled on a pair of boxers and climbed in bed. He allowed himself an hour of thinking about Jacky and what it was like to have someone hold him in bed before he closed his eyes and let the weariness of the day catch up with him. He had to go back to the way things were—he had no choice.

# CHAPTER TWO

SIMON and Gardner packed up and left the hotel soon after Gardner arrived in the morning with a huge smile on his face and a pleasant mood that lasted the entire three-hour drive home. "You're especially pensive," Gardner observed as they neared home. "You haven't said two words the entire trip. I would have thought you'd be chattering away about your performance yesterday, or at the very least about being able to sit down and talk with Dante Rivers. You should be thrilled."

"I am," Simon said. "I've just got some things to think about."

"Like the fact that your mother will skin you alive if she finds out where you were," Gardner supplied, and Simon nodded. That was as good an excuse as any for the way he was acting. "You know it will be okay. She might get mad, but in the end you're an adult and you can live your own life. Besides, you're pretty good. You couldn't have ridden that bull if you weren't."

"Dante said the same thing when he wasn't teasing me." He wished he'd had the opportunity to ask Dante if he really thought Simon's ride had just been luck or if there was more to it. But he hadn't gotten the chance. That wasn't what was bothering him, though. It was just a good distraction from the real issue—*the big issue*. "Not that it really matters. I can only get to a few rodeos a year without making my folks suspicious, so it isn't like I'll ever really have the chance to get the experience to reach the top anyway. This is only something I can do for fun and nothing more."

"Dude, I saw you ride. I saw the look on your face. You're happier when you're about to ride than I've ever seen you. I feel the same way about broncs. If my dad told me I couldn't ride or some crap like that, I'd tell him good-bye," Gardner said and sat back in his seat like he'd just spoken the word of God.

"That's easy for you to say. You know who my folks are. Do you think they'll just let me do whatever I want?"

"It's only rodeo. Sure, they'll freak a little. You think my dad didn't? But they'll get over it and then call you after every ride to make sure you're okay. Just tell them what you want. Be honest with them and they'll appreciate it. If they find out on their own, they'll be doubly angry."

Gardner had a point. Maybe Simon should come clean, at least about the bull riding. He'd won some money this weekend. Maybe now was a good time to explain what he wanted to do. Sure, his mom would freak, but there were worse things, and there was definitely worse news he could give them.

"Maybe you're right," Simon agreed as he came to the small ranch where Gardner lived with his dad. He slowed and pulled down the drive, then parked in front of the house.

"How'd you do?" Gardner's dad, Milt, asked. He must have been watching for them—he came out to meet them just as the truck pulled to a stop.

"We both ended up in the money. Frizz came in second, and I made enough to pay for my share of the trip and gas, plus a little, so it was good. How are things here?"

"Quiet, as usual," Milt answered with a beaming smile of pride. Simon often wished he'd see that look on his folks' faces, but they had very different priorities than Milt. "So you had a good couple rides," Milt said, turning to Simon.

"Yeah, he did, and guess who was there—Dante Rivers. He saw Frizz ride and told him he'd done good. He teased him a little at first, but they even got a chance to talk when we saw them at the bar last night. He seems like a good guy." Gardner was laying it on a bit thick after what he'd said the night before, but Simon kept quiet.

"Wasn't he world champion?" Milt asked.

"Yes. They were on vacation in the area and stopped in to see the rodeo. He even rode one of the bulls in the show. God, you should have seen him. All the other guys were just trying to get the job done and Dante made it look almost poetic, like he could read that beast's mind. It was amazing."

"I bet it was," Milt said. "Now both of you come on inside. I got some lunch on, and then you can head on home."

"Thanks," Simon said. Gardner went on inside, and Milt hung back with him.

"You need to tell your folks what you're doing and what you want. I know they won't cotton to it at first, but they need to know you're riding rodeo, and you need to be the one to tell 'em. They worry, and…." Milt sighed. "Son, you gotta think of the other people who know. If your folks find out you've been keeping secrets and other people have been helping you, there'll be hell to pay, and not just for you. Your mama and daddy are good folks, but when your daddy gets riled up, you know how he can be. All scorched earth."

"I know. Gardner and I were talking 'bout that on the way home. I figured since I came in the money, now might be a good time to tell them. Mama gets all worried, and Daddy says it's no way to make a proper living, but it's what I love," Simon explained, and Milt smiled.

"I know it is, kid. I done it when I was your age. Got the buckles to prove it, and the bum knee." Milt smiled and motioned toward the house. "Let's go in and eat. You can think on what you want to do and fill your stomach at the same time." Milt led the way inside. "There's one good thing about riding rodeo. If you were a jockey you'd have to watch every calorie you ate." They found Gardner in the kitchen making what he called mile-high sandwiches. There must have been half a million calories in each one, and they all ate them without thinking.

Once all three of them were full, Milt went out to get chores done, and Gardner walked Simon to the truck. "I'll call you, and we'll see when we can go again."

Simon nodded. "I'm going to tell my folks what I want to do. My mom will have a fit, and who knows how my dad will react."

"You've always got a place here, man," Gardner said. "No matter what. We're brothers, and you're always welcome here." Gardner bro-hugged him and then walked toward the barn. "You better go before Dad decides you're staying and makes you muck out stalls." Gardner laughed as he lifted Simon's gear out of the back of the truck to stow it for him. Simon raised his hand in good-bye and thank-you before getting in the truck and driving toward home.

The half-hour drive went by more quickly than usual, and soon Simon turned down the drive. The house was easily visible from the road and looked like it would be much more at home in Kentucky than in Oklahoma with its red brick, white pillars, and rolling grasslands in front divided into neat paddocks with white-painted fences. Simon's mother had been born and raised in Kentucky, and she adored horses as long as they were for dressage, hunt, chase, or some other sport she considered socially acceptable and elegantly genteel. He rode up to the house and parked in a spot behind the other cars before grabbing his bag of clothes and heading inside.

The house was unusually quiet when Simon entered. He heard a few voices coming from the hall, but he wasn't in the mood to talk, so he used the back stairs, climbed up to the second floor, and then went down the hall to his room. Inside, he put his dirty clothes in the hamper in his bathroom and then used the quiet time to take a shower.

By the time he was clean and dressed, he heard more sounds in the house, so he left his room, descending the stairs to the family room. His parents as well as his seven younger brothers and sisters were still in their Sunday clothes when he walked in.

"Did you have a nice time?" his mother asked before kissing him lightly on the cheek. "I'm assuming you went to church as part of your retreat."

"That's what I wanted to talk to you and Dad about," Simon said, and his mother lifted her eyebrows but didn't say anything to him.

"Go on upstairs and get out of those clothes," his mother told the kids, and they tramped out of the room and ran upstairs like a herd of elephants.

"Let me change and we can talk," his father said before climbing the stairs. His mother followed, and Simon was left alone in the large room, but not for long. His youngest sister, three-year-old Miriam, rushed in wearing misbuttoned pants, a pair of pink socks clutched in her hands. She bounded up on the sofa and jumped into Simon's arms. "Simon, help me," she said with a giggle as she waved the socks in the air.

"Okay, ya squirmy monster," Simon said as he set her down on the sofa. He tickled her before getting her socks on. Then he stood her up and finished buttoning her pants. "There you are," he said with a smile. "Now go get some shoes before Mama has a fit."

She stomped once. "I hate shoes," she said indignantly.

"I know, but that will change, I'm sure," he said before scooting her out of the room toward the stairs. She ran up as the others began trickling down. In his family, Sunday was taken very seriously as a day of rest. His mother usually cooked a grand meal. Family activities and games were usually planned, and his father never went into the office.

The television switched on as Jeremiah and Malachi bounded into the room. They were twelve-year-old twins, and the most boisterous in the family. They also seemed to share one mind, even if they also went out of their way to differentiate themselves from the other. They fired up the video game console and immediately involved themselves in a game that Simon was willing to bet his parents hadn't realized had made its way into the house. The figures were in battle fatigues, shooting and blowing up enemy soldiers. "You better not let Mom see that," Simon whispered, and they looked up at him and nodded before returning to the game.

"Gross," Jeremiah said with a touch of awed reverence. "That'll teach you," he added before blowing up another enemy, body parts flying around the screen.

"This is so cool," Malachi whispered as they kept playing.

Simon left the room. He wasn't about to get caught up in the drama that would inevitably erupt when his mother caught them. Simon wandered to his father's home office and sat down to wait for him. Miriam ran in and climbed on his lap. "Are you in trouble?" she asked, peering up at him with her huge blue eyes.

"I don't think so," he told her.

"Then why are you sitting in the naughty chair?" she asked. "Just say you're sorry."

"Simon hasn't done anything," his father said as he strode into the room. "He just wants to talk to us." He plucked Miriam off Simon's lap and lifted her into the air. Miriam giggled with glee as their father flew her around the room until Simon's mother joined them. "Go on and play. Simon will be out soon, and I promise, no one's in trouble." She hurried out, and his father closed the door. "What is it you want to talk about?" His father sat on the leather sofa next to his mother, which left him in the hot seat.

He wasn't sure where to start. For a second, the night before came flooding back and the words to tell them everything were on the tip of his tongue, but there was no way he was ready for that, let alone them. "I need to come clean about something. I wasn't at a retreat this weekend. I was at a rodeo."

"I don't understand. Why didn't you say you wanted to go?" his father began and then stopped. "You didn't just watch the rodeo, did you?"

"No," Simon answered. "I was there to compete."

"After we forbade it," his mother said.

"Martha, it's okay," his father said. "I don't condone you going against the rules your mother and I set down, but you came forward with the truth. Now that you've got this out of your system—"

"Dad, that wasn't the first time," Simon cut in. "I've ridden in six rodeos, and each time I get better. Yesterday I came in second." Simon showed his father the check he'd won. "This is what I want to do. I love it and I want to be able to train properly. I hated lying about it, but I think I'm good. I had two good rides, and the last one was on a ranked bull."

"You were riding those death traps?" his mother cried. "We forbid you to ride, and you do it anyway. What are we going to do? Because you certainly aren't going to be riding again."

"Martha," his father soothed. "He's a man and he can make his own decisions. I wish you'd discussed it with us before you went behind our backs. You need to find your own way. I don't cotton to lying, but I'm grateful you told us."

"How can you be so calm about this?" his mother asked.

"Because I've seen it coming. When he was a kid, he was fascinated watching the others ride. I knew he wanted his chance. We raise our children and instill in them the values we hope they'll carry into adulthood. Beyond that they need to make their own decisions." His father was the only person on earth who could calm his mother once she got in one of her obstinate moods. "But that's not to say we're happy about this. What you want to do is dangerous. People get injured or killed."

"I know," Simon said. "But I love it. I always wear a protective vest, and I'll even wear one of the helmets instead of a cowboy hat if you want, but I really want to do this." He could tell his father was on his side, but he had to sway his mother. "I know you're scared, Mom, but I can do this and I can be really good at it. I know it." Simon swallowed. "I was never good at anything. In school, I barely made it through. Everyone's good at something—maybe this is it for me. If I wait any longer, I'll be too old."

His mother shifted her gaze to Simon's dad. "You know how I feel about this," she said.

"Yes, I do," his father agreed. "But we weren't given children to stand in their way or to govern them by our own fears. Each person must make his way in this world. You and I did, and Simon has to as well." His father turned to him even as he took his mother's hand. "You'll need to find someone who's willing to work with you. I'll give you a career path in one of the stores, but that's all I can do. You know the book business and have always been a hard worker, so any of the managers would be pleased to have you. But…." His father paused. "You'll have to work for anything more. There will be no allowances and no calls home for money. If this doesn't work out, you can come into the business and work with me, but at that point, there will be no more talk of rodeo. I'm not convinced this is a viable way to make a living, but you're asking for a chance, so we'll give it to you."

"Thank you," Simon said as he stood up. "Thank you both," he added and then hugged his mother. "I know this scares you, but I have to try."

Then he hugged his father.

"I meant what I said," his father said.

"I know, Dad," Simon told him.

"So if you do this, I suggest you start looking for a place you can work and train."

Simon nodded before leaving the room. His parents didn't get up, and Simon closed the door. He knew they'd continue talking and that his father would spend some time calming his mother's fears.

His dad had said he'd give him a job in one of the stores, but he hadn't agreed to sponsor him. Training for bull riding wasn't cheap. It required equipment and access to bulls, as well as event entrance fees, travel, food, and God knew what else. At least he had their permission—that was a start. Now he needed to figure out how come up with the rest. Simon joined the kids in the family room, and his mother came in a few minutes later to tell them all she was starting dinner.

He sat for a while and then left the room to call Gardner.

"I told you it would be okay," Gardner said as soon as Simon had told him how it went with his folks. "Now it sounds like you need a sponsor, but in order to get one, you need to go to rodeos so you can be seen."

"Exactly. No one is going to sponsor a nobody," Simon said. "But at least I have the money I won. I can put that aside, and if I'm careful I can use it to go to two rodeos. And if I have good rides, I may be able to win more."

"And if you don't…," Gardner prompted.

"Then I get to spend the rest of my life behind the counter of one of Frizzell's Family Bookstores. Joy of joys." His father and mother had opened a single bookstore just after they were married. They'd specialized in what they said were "family books," with a large section of Christian and spiritual studies. The store was a success, and they'd opened a second and then a third store. Now there were almost three dozen all over the South and West. The rise of Amazon had worried his father, but that hadn't touched their business, and their customer base kept growing, especially since the family supported churches and family-based organizations in all the towns they served, guaranteeing a fiercely loyal clientele. "The last thing I want is to spend my life working in one of the stores. Dad keeps hoping I'll come work for him."

"Okay, so what's the plan?"

"Don't know. What I need is someone to work with, bulls to ride, training, stuff like that. There's no one around here with any of that stuff. Your daddy's got broncs and you can train with them, but no one around here has bulls. Sneaking off to use mechanical bulls isn't going to cut it long term."

"Try the Internet," Gardner suggested. "You could probably get a job on a ranch somewhere. You got plenty of experience with horses and cattle from working around your place and helping at ours. Ya know, you could contact Dante Rivers. He saw you ride, and you met him at the bar. He might know a place where you can train and stuff. He's plugged into the whole circuit."

"I'm sure he is. But I can't just call him up and ask him for help. I just met him that one time," Simon said, wishing he'd had the presence of mind to get Jacky's phone number. Jacky was friends with Dante and maybe he could help. Somehow Simon got the feeling that researching job prospects might be outside the realm of a one-night stand.

"I bet if you researched him on the Internet, you could come up with an e-mail address. Send a message. The worst he could do is say no or not reply," Gardner said, and Simon heard someone calling in the background. "I gotta go. Call me when you decide what you want to do." He hung up, and Simon shoved his phone back in his pocket.

Gardner's idea wasn't too harebrained, and he was right, the worst Dante could do was ignore him, so Simon went up to his room and powered up his computer. It took a while to boot up and then he logged on to the Internet.

It turned out Dante had a website with an e-mail address, so Simon copied in the address and sat in front of a blank e-mail screen, wondering what in the hell to say. He wanted the note to sound professional, so he started with how nice it had been to meet him at the rodeo. He also thanked him for the drink and then got down to business. He must have typed and deleted most of the main part of the note half a dozen times before he settled on wording that didn't sound really dumb or like he was begging. He asked for advice and if Dante knew of someone with bulls who was hiring. Simon explained about his ranch experience and ended with a nice closing about appreciating Dante's time. He also included his address and telephone number to show he wasn't some crackpot.

Simon read the note over again and again, and changed a few words before finally deciding it was as good as it was going to get. Then he held his breath and pressed the send button. Of course, the message was sent and then nothing happened. Simon laughed at himself and got up from the computer. Then he went downstairs and decided to go for a ride to try to clear his head. As soon as he mentioned it to his parents, the kids all decided it was a good idea, and Simon ended up out in the barn helping the younger kids with their horses and ponies. Miriam went with him, and Simon ended up leading a "trail" ride around the ranch. They never actually left the enclosed areas, but the terrain changed enough that the kids were happy. The twins took off on their own, which was fine. They tended to push Danny and Eve, who at ages eight and seven were still learning to control their ponies, so speed wasn't the goal as much as practice and having fun. Ruth, who was two years younger than Simon, rode with five-year-old Solomon.

"Are you ready to go in?" Simon asked Miriam, but she shook her head.

"Wanna go fast," she said. "Go, horsie, go," she encouraged, but Simon kept his mount steady.

"Maybe when you're a little older you can go faster," he told her and pointed them back toward the barn. Ruth, Danny, and Eve followed him, and soon their little caravan entered the yard. Simon's mother met them, and Simon handed her Miriam before dismounting and leading his horse inside. Simon got Brook settled before helping the other two kids with their ponies. They did pretty well but were still young enough that Simon had to make sure they didn't forget anything and that their ponies were settled and happy before letting them go back to the house. Then Simon took care of Brook, brushing him down and making sure he had hay and water before heading inside himself. The first thing he did was check his e-mail, but there was nothing, so he cleaned up to get ready for dinner.

SIMON checked his e-mail every few hours for days. Of course, as time passed he began to give up hope and scoured the Internet for ranches that raised bucking bulls and began contacting them. The answer he received was always the same: they had plenty of help and weren't interested in taking on anyone new. Some of them were impressed by his qualifications, but they simply weren't hiring. He even tried going farther afield, but he always seemed to get the same answer, and the farther away he got, the less receptive people were.

"I'm not sure what to do, Milt," Simon told Mr. Gardner one evening during the week when he needed someone he could talk to. "They actually gave me their blessing, but I need a place I can train, and I can't get near one."

"I know. I've been giving it some thought, and I keep coming up with nothing. There isn't a place around here that has what you need. There used to be a bar about an hour away with one of those mechanical bulls, but they closed years ago. I called around to see if the machine might still be around, but no one thinks so."

"Thanks," Simon said. "I guess all I can do is try to get to some events and hope I can get people to take notice."

"Then things will fall in your lap?" Milt asked. "Come on, Simon. Most things in your life have come easily to you. Your folks are big fish in this part of the state. Once people find out who you are, the way forward seems to open easily." Milt put his hand up when Simon opened his mouth. "I know you've kept who you are quiet and I applaud that, but that doesn't change the fact that you expect things to come to you. This is something you're going to have to work for and pay your dues like everyone else. I'll keep my ears to the ground. Sometimes things come my way, but I suspect you're going to need to work hard, ride well, and trust a bit to luck like the rest of us." Milt lightly squeezed Simon's shoulder. "You're a good kid, but sometimes I think you were given too much. Whatever happens with this, work hard at it."

Simon stared at Milt. "Was I that bad?"

Milt laughed. "No. You were better behaved than Billy Bob was. It's just that sometimes I worried you got things too easily. If something is worth having, it's worth working for. I know you know that. So throw yourself into what you want to do. Don't worry about winning or losing, just do your best. As long as you do that, good things will happen, and if they don't, you're blessed with a family and friends here who care for you. That's a lot more than most people have." Simon could always count on Milt to provide down-to earth advice. "Now I gotta finish up for the night, and I suspect you and my son were expecting to have some fun this evening."

They had planned to go out, but Simon wasn't in the mood. He wanted to do something to get his rodeo career moving, but felt stymied, and going out drinking wouldn't help things. Besides, if his mother found out, she wouldn't be particularly happy. Simon and his mother had very different attitudes about a lot of things. To her, alcohol was some sort of demon. They kept none in the house and never had. Even his father had to leave if he wanted a sip of whiskey, although Simon figured there might be a bottle hidden in one of the locked drawers in his dad's office. But in most ways, his mother was supportive and caring. Lord knew she could be a tigress if she thought one of her children was in danger or hurt. Maybe those were just two sides of the same coin.

"Are you ready to go?" Gardner asked as he strode up to where Simon had been absently watching the horses.

"I don't think I'm in the mood," Simon said.

"Come on. The place will be packed with girls. Tonight Chappy's has a live band, and that always brings out the honeys. A little dancing, a little liquid lubrication, and…."

"You go on if you want," Simon told him. "I'm not in the mood for liquid lubrication. I gotta figure out what I'm going to do. Can you believe I got my folks' support and I can't find a job anywhere? Maybe I should go work in one of the stores down in Texas. At least I'd be closer to where the action is and might be able to find a position."

"You're going to leave? Of course you gotta leave. There's nothing around here except your friends and family," he groused.

"I've tried getting a job around here, but no one has bulls like that. I contacted a bunch of places, but no one's hiring, so I gotta go where the action is. It's not like I'm never going to see you. We'll still enter and travel together. That is, if you want to."

Gardner put his arm around Simon's shoulders. "Of course I do. I just hadn't thought through the fact that I might be losing my best friend and stuff."

"You aren't losing anything. God, you sound like a girl," Simon teased and took off across the field with Gardner right behind him. Simon had always been just a little faster, so he pulled away and then turned back toward the house.

"I'll show you who sounds like a girl," Gardner called as Simon miscalculated. Gardner lunged and caught him around the waist. They both went tumbling on the ground, laughing like idiots.

"It's so easy to wind you up," Simon said, and Gardner picked up his hat, swatting Simon with it before getting to his feet.

"Come on. If you don't want to go out, then we need to find you a place with some bulls to ride." Gardner grinned, and they headed inside.

MOST of the places they found, Simon had already contacted. He did find a few new possibilities and made a note to send off inquiries, but he wasn't hopeful. Doubts nagged at him, but Milt's words kept him going. When he got home, Simon checked his e-mail—nothing—and sent off the inquiries before going to bed.

He woke bright and early and went down to the barn to take his frustrations out with some good old-fashioned work. He hauled hay bales, cleaned a few stalls, and then swept the barn. By the time he was done, Simon had sweated through his shirt and was hungry as hell. He walked back to the house and was met by Miriam, who was carrying his phone. "It ringed, Simon," she said and lifted it up to him.

"Thank you," he told her as he bent down to take the phone. He saw he'd missed a call.

"Ewww, stinky," she pronounced and handed him the phone before running toward the kitchen. "Mama, Simon is stinkypoo."

He chuckled and climbed the stairs on his way to his room. Inside, with the door closed, he set his phone on the dresser and stripped off his clothes before he went into his private bathroom and locked the door behind him; habit after growing up with a passel of younger siblings. Simon started the water and stepped into the shower. Instantly, the tension melted from his body. He'd been worrying and going at a fast pace for days. Leaning back against the cool tiled wall, he let his mind wander, and within seconds, a smile shone behind his closed eyes. Jacky. He'd played a starring role in Simon's dreams for days and had awakened things Simon wasn't sure he knew how to handle. It had always been easy to ignore other guys because he'd managed to keep his feelings under tight control. But now that he'd let them out once, they weren't as easy to subdue, and he found himself looking more than he should. Simon slid his hand down his stomach and then along his shaft, which was pointing toward the ceiling as he remembered how Jacky had looked at him and the way his skin had burned and he'd come alive under his touch. Simon gripped himself and began stroking, running his finger over the head of his cock, pretending it was Jacky's lips and tongue making his legs shake and his breath hitch.

"Simon!" Miriam shouted through the bathroom door. "Your phone is playing music again."

He peeked out from behind the curtain. "Okay. I'll get it in a minute," he called back and glanced at the door, thankful he'd remembered to lock it. He took a deep breath and sighed before turning off the water and grabbing for a towel. He dried himself quickly and then wrapped the towel around his waist before opening the door and peering into his bedroom. Miriam sat on the side of his bed, staring at his phone on the dresser. "Go on and let me change."

"Is your phone going to ring again? I like the music it plays," Miriam said, and Simon shook his head. Sometimes she was fascinated by the strangest things.

"I don't know. But let me change clothes, and after I return the calls, I'll see if I can't find you a copy of the ringtone that you can play all you want."

"Okay," she said happily and turned around before sliding off the bed and skipping out of the room. Simon closed the door and dressed quickly. He checked his e-mail, like he'd been doing for the last few days, and then picked up his phone and listened to his voice mail.

"This is Ryan Abbott, Dante Rivers's partner, and I got your e-mail. Please return my call." He gave a number, and Simon rushed to write it down. Then he returned the call.

"Ryan Abbott."

"Umm, this is Simon Frizzell. You called and left me a message about the e-mail I sent Dante."

"Yeah, Frizz, it took me a few minutes to make the connection when I saw your message. So you're looking for a job and you want to ride," Ryan said. "In your note you said you had ranch experience."

"Yes. My folks have horses, and if you remember Gardner, the guy I was with, his family has a cattle ranch, so I've done lots of ranch work and I know what's involved."

"From your last name, I'll also assume you know your way around a bookstore," Ryan said.

"Yeah, well, I try to keep that part quiet. I want folks to take me seriously for the riding and not because they think I've got lots of money," Simon explained.

"That's admirable," Ryan said. "We have a ranch about an hour or so outside Houston. It's been in Dante's family for a long time. Now that he's retired, he's decided to grow the ranch and we need some help. I have no idea if Dante will want to work with you or not. He gets touchy about riding sometimes, so that part is up to you. But as long as you can pull your weight, you have a job if you want it. The other stuff is up to you."

"Thanks." Simon beamed into the phone. They talked for a few minutes more, settling on when Simon should come, salary, and other details. By the time he hung up, Simon's face hurt from smiling. He set the phone back on the dresser and stopped himself from letting out the whoop he felt in his heart. He and Ryan had agreed he'd be at their place and ready to work in a week. Ryan provided Simon with directions and a variety of other details. The one thing that bothered Simon was the part about Dante and riding, but he figured he could see how that went. Dante had been a world champion and he still rode bulls, so he must train to keep in shape and his skills honed. He figured he'd worry about that part once he got there.

Simon stepped out of his room and found Miriam playing with one of her dolls on the hallway floor. "Come on, silly puss," he said, scooping her into his arms. "Let's get you a copy of that song, and then you and I can tell Mama and Daddy that I got a job." Simon swung her around, and she giggled, filling the entire area with laughter that exactly echoed Simon's excitement.

Simon found his father sitting in his office, staring dourly out the window. "Go on and play with the other kids," Simon told Miriam, and he set her on her feet. She looked at both of them and ran from the room, calling out to the other kids.

"I got a job, Dad," Simon said, and his dad slowly turned toward him. "I have an offer of a job at a ranch outside Houston. They want me to start in about a week. I'll have the opportunity to ride and work with someone with experience." Some of Simon's excitement evaporated when he saw the turmoil in his father's eyes. "What is it?"

His father cleared his throat slightly and he motioned toward the chair next to him. "I was hoping you'd changed your mind. I have an opening for a manager in one of the stores in Oklahoma City, and I was hoping you'd take it." He still sounded distracted and concerned.

"I thought you had a full complement of trusted managers. Most of them have been with you for years," Simon said.

His father nodded. "This is very disconcerting, but we had to let one of our managers go. I've been able to promote an experienced assistant manager to the job, which leaves an opening you could fill. It could be the start of your career in the business. I'd love to have you work with me."

Simon was about to thank his father and decline, but his father's expression stopped him. Something was really bothering him. Simon rarely saw his father flustered. As far as he knew, Simon's father had everything he wanted and had always seemed happy and contented. Maybe that was a face he put on for the family, but Simon didn't think so. Something had really rattled his dad. "What's really bothering you?" Simon asked softly.

"Close the door. I don't want your mother to know," his dad said, and Simon slowly got up and shut the office door. Simon had never thought about his father keeping secrets from his mother, and this turn of events bothered him. "As you said, our managers often stay with us. Your mother and I started the business on a few basic principles, like only stocking family and Christian books, and we promised ourselves that our workers would be like family. So we provide insurance to our workers and treat them well. In return, they have all helped make the business better, and in the end, we've been more successful than we ever imagined. Other bookstores have closed, but we're still going strong."

"I know. So what changed?" Simon asked,

"The manager in the Oklahoma City store had been with us for over five years. I had lunch with him the last time I visited the store. He called me two months ago and explained that he needed some time off. He was distraught. He said a friend of his had passed away and he needed to help the family through their grief. I, of course, gave him the time off. The thing is, I found out shortly afterwards that his 'friend' was his gay lover. He was having some… affair with another man." His father shivered. "I prayed about what to do, and in the end I had to let him go. I couldn't have someone like that working in our stores. We have children's story time, and what if he…." His dad shivered again, but it was Simon who went completely cold inside.

"You fired him for being gay?" Simon whispered. The subject of gay people rarely came up in their house, but Simon had heard plenty of condemnation from the minister at church.

"No," his dad said hastily. "I don't want to be the next Chick-Fil-A. I found another reason, but I had to let him go. Last week the store came up short, and I…."

Simon didn't need to hear anything more. His father had found an excuse and fired the man for being gay. He took a deep breath and then released it slowly as he wondered what his dad would do if he knew about him and what he'd done with Jacky. Would his dad fire him as his son? Should he just take the job with his dad? If he did, at least he'd be away from further temptation at a ranch with gay men, but he'd also be giving up his dream.

His father seemed to brighten after a few seconds. "I'm happy for you," he said with a smile. "And it was probably wrong of me to burden you with this. You take the job at the ranch and go after what you want. It's not right for me to push you into a job that isn't what you want. Your mother and I have worked hard to provide opportunities to our children that we never had." His father smiled broadly. "When I was a kid, I wanted to be a jockey and race horses. I loved the feel of flying over the land, just me and the horse. I trained and rode every chance I got."

"What happened?"

"I grew and then grew some more," his dad said with a chuckle. "I got too big to be competitive. But I never lost the love. I probably could have done something else, but that was my dream and I couldn't have it." His father sighed softly. "As much as your dream scares both me and your mother, we won't stand in your way. There will be other stores and other positions." He stood up, and Simon did the same. "I'm proud of you. You stuck with it and found a job on your own." His father hugged him, and Simon wondered just how proud his father would be if he knew where Simon was going.

"So who are you going to work for?" his father asked.

"Ryan Abbott," Simon answered. He almost said "Dante Rivers," but stopped himself. Dante's name was too well known, and Ryan was the person who had called and offered him the job. If Gardner knew about Dante, then his father could easily find out, but no one was likely to recognize Ryan's name. "He hired me for his ranch, and they have a retired bull rider there, so I'm hoping I can work with him." Simon chose his words carefully. He didn't want to lie, and what he'd said was the truth, but he wouldn't provide any information he didn't have to.

"Have you heard of these people?" Simon's father sounded full of fatherly concern.

"Yes, I've met them at rodeos," Simon said, and then he wished he hadn't reminded his father of his earlier deception. "They're good people with a good reputation for having quality stock." That much he knew. "I'll be fine. It's time I made my own way. I know you and Mom are there for me." Even as he said the words, he wondered if they would be if they knew the whole story. Simon forced a smile and left the office.

AFTER telling his mother the news, and receiving a definitely mixed reaction, Simon spent much of the week packing his things and getting ready to go to his new job. He didn't figure he needed furniture, but he wanted to take his clothes and gear, along with a few other things. The trip would take about eight hours, so Simon figured he'd drive straight through. He'd get an early start—the last thing he wanted to do was be late. Ryan had told him to call when he left so he'd have an idea when Simon would be arriving.

The night before he was supposed to leave, Simon's mother made him a special dinner, and the entire family gathered together to celebrate the first of the children leaving the nest. His mother still wasn't keen on the reason he was leaving, but she was his mom, and while she never said she understood, she cooked up a storm, showing love the way she always had to all of them—with food. The meal was raucous and loud, just as Simon expected, and it ended with Jeremiah asking if he could have Simon's room. Before he could answer, Simon's mother told him no. He was going to continue to share a room with his twin and that seemed final.

Simon shrugged, and his mother brought out chocolate cake, his favorite. For a few seconds, Simon wondered if she thought he was going to jail or to his death or something. Maybe in the back of her mind that was what she was afraid of, after what had happened to her brother. "Mom, I'm going to be fine," Simon told her, taking her hand. She smiled at him slightly, but he could tell she wasn't convinced. "I am, Mom."

"He's only taking a job," his dad said soothingly.

"No, he's not. He's going to be riding bulls…."

"Simon is going to be fine," his father said and took her other hand in his. "It's what he wants to do. We always said that whatever skills the good Lord gave our children, we'd nurture and encourage them. That's what we're doing." His dad didn't seem as convinced as he'd sounded earlier, and Simon lowered his gaze to his cake and slowly began to eat. He was both excited and scared. He was leaving home to take a job five hundred miles away. Mom and Dad wouldn't be there to bail him out or take care of things. He would be on his own.

After dinner, everyone did their usual thing. Simon ended up in the family room playing video games, without the guns and explosions this time. Apparently their mother had confiscated that disk, much to the twins' consternation and backside discomfort.

"Are you sad?" Miriam asked as she climbed on his lap between games. Solomon, who was five, wanted up too, so Simon ended up with one on each knee.

"No, I'm just thinking," Simon told her.

"You looked sad," she pressed, and Solomon nodded. They'd already diagnosed that Solomon had a developmental delay, so even at five, he didn't talk much.

"I'm a little sad that I won't be able to see you two as much," he said, hugging both kids, covering up what was really bothering him. He was excited about leaving home and being on his own for a while, but he kept coming back to the conversation he'd had with his father a week ago. He'd played it over and over in his mind, thankful he'd kept his mouth shut. Through that same period, he'd done his best to block out what had happened between him and Jacky. When he went to the ranch, he had to concentrate on his work and not on the sins of the flesh. He somehow had to put those thoughts from his mind and work toward his goal. That was why he was there, to become a better bull rider and start a life of his own. He wasn't there to get a boyfriend or to sleep around with other guys. He needed to keep his eyes on the prize and let the rest of it go.

"You still sad," Miriam said, and Simon hugged both kids again before lowering them to the floor and starting a tickle fight that ended up with all the littler kids on top of him in a writhing, giggling, squirming, laughing pile. It was just what he needed.

After they'd gotten up, his mother came in to put the youngest ones to bed. Simon helped her, and both Solomon and Miriam asked for a rodeo story before he left. He told them about rodeo clowns, roping steers, and barrel riders who moved so fast you could hardly see them. The kids laughed, and even his mother smiled slightly. Then he took Miriam to her room and put her to bed while his mother did the same for Solomon. His father came up and said good night. Simon left the room to give him some night-night time with the kids. He made sure he had everything packed and ready before joining the others in the family room.

When it was time for the others to go to bed, Simon went to bed as well. He had to get up early, even for him, to get on the road. He said good night to his parents, went to his room, and closed the door.

He got ready for bed and was about to climb under the covers when he heard a soft knock on the door. "Yes?" he said softly. The door opened and his mother peered inside. "Hey, Mom."

She stepped inside. "You know I'm not happy about what you're doing, but I'm proud of you for deciding to make your own way. I know I won't always agree with your decisions, and this is hard for me." She pulled a tissue out of her sleeve, where she always kept one. "My baby is growing up. I know you'll make us proud."

"I will, Mom," Simon said, and she turned back toward the door. "I really want this."

"I know," she said with her hand on the doorknob. "Don't forget to find a church near that ranch. I don't want you spending every Sunday sleeping off Saturday night, and who knows, you might meet a nice girl who catches your eye."

"Mom, you know I don't act like that," Simon told her.

She nodded. "Just so you remember how to behave. The other men might not act like it, but you were brought up right, and people should know that. Always say please and thank you, and no matter what anybody says, the place to meet girls is not in some bar or at a club, but in church, because that's where you'll meet the ones worth marrying."

"I know, Mom," Simon told her. Not that he was interested in meeting any girls to marry or for anything other than friends.

"I met your father in church," she said.

"I know, Mom," Simon repeated. "Is all this your way of saying you want grandchildren?"

"Heavens, no," she said, putting her hand over her chest. "I'm too young, and so are you. Meet a nice girl, get married, and then think about children, preferably not before I've got the youngest of my own in school. There's no rush, believe me." She smiled and walked back to where Simon sat on the edge of the bed. Leaning down, she lightly kissed his forehead. "Behave and work hard."

"I'll make you proud," he said.

"You already have," she said and then left the room. Simon swallowed around the lump in his throat as the door clicked closed. Somehow he doubted she'd still be proud of him if she knew everything about him. Simon's resolution steeled inside him, and he turned out the light and climbed into bed.

He didn't sleep well at all and spent most of the night either staring at the ceiling or rolling over until the covers puddled on the floor. Sleep stayed away no matter what he did. A few times he closed his eyes and thought the clock next to the bed had jumped ahead, but he was never sure. By the time the windows lightened, Simon was up and out of bed, his excitement carrying him into the day. He cleaned up and loaded everything in his truck. By the time he was ready to go, his father was up, and Simon said good-bye before climbing in the truck and heading toward the highway. He stopped for lunch and a couple of bathroom breaks. Hour after hour of nothing to see passed outside his windows. Finally, after passing out of Oklahoma and through northern Texas, he approached his destination. Simon pulled off and called Ryan to confirm his directions and then drove the last hour to the ranch.

By the time he pulled into the drive, Simon was exhausted. He'd barely slept the night before, then he'd spent the entire day driving. He pulled up to the house and put the truck in park, slumping over the wheel once the engine quieted.

"Are you okay?" A tap on the window caught Simon's attention, and he straightened up. "Frizz?" Jacky stared at him through the glass and broke into a huge smile.

Instantly, the fatigue vanished, and Simon smiled back. Jacky opened the door, and Simon got out of the truck.

"You made it," Ryan said as he came out of the house.

"Why didn't you tell me the new guy you hired was Frizz?" Jacky asked Ryan without looking away from him, and Simon squirmed slightly under the intense attention.

Ryan ignored the question. "Why don't you come inside? I've been expecting you. We have a room for you in the house until we can settle things in the bunkhouse. It isn't very large, but I hope it will do for you." Ryan stepped aside, and Simon got some of his things and carried them inside. Jacky grabbed some things as well and followed behind. "You aren't expected to start work until Monday."

"I can help tomorrow if you need it," Simon volunteered as he walked into the room Ryan showed him.

"How about you learn where things are and explore a bit. I'm sure we keep things differently here. Besides, tomorrow's Sunday, and that's a light workday. We do the chores we need to and then most of the men have the afternoon and evening free. Dinner will be in about an hour, so get settled and come out when you're ready." Ryan left, and Simon began putting his things away, trying his best to keep his attention and interest off Jacky. He had to be strong.

"I need to finish getting unpacked," Simon said softly. Part of him wanted Jacky to leave, and part of him, the part that made his heart pound and his blood race, very much wanted Jacky to stay.

Jacky touched his arm, and Simon turned toward him. "I've thought about you for weeks," Jacky said. "Ever since I woke alone in that hotel room, I've thought about you."

"I've thought about you too," Simon admitted in a whisper. He could feel the resolve he'd built all along the drive begin to crumble.

"I should let you get settled," Jacky said and then stepped closer. He touched Simon's chin, and Simon stopped what he was doing and lifted his gaze. Jacky leaned closer and kissed him. In that instant, the bulwark he thought he'd built out of stone turned to sand and crumbled.

"I shouldn't do this," Simon said as he backed away and took a deep breath. "I need to finish unpacking." He turned away. By the time he looked again, Jacky had left the room. Simon's lips still tingled as he finished unpacking and then sat on the end of the bed. The room was nothing like what he had at home. It was much plainer than the one his mother had decorated for him, but he was here and on his own.

"Dinner will be ready soon," Ryan said from the doorway.

"Thank you so much," Simon said with a smile, and Ryan hesitated before leaving. After a few seconds, Simon stood up and left the room, then walked through the house to the kitchen. He found Jacky sitting at the table and sat down across from him. He had a new job and a chance to start a life of his own. Now he had to figure out what he wanted to do with that chance, and dang if the decision didn't get harder every time he looked up from the table and saw Jacky's eyes and smile. Doing the right thing would be really hard, but he'd promised himself. He needed to keep his mind on his job and what he'd come here for. Simon swallowed, and he watched Jacky watch him. His heart thumped so loudly he could hear it, and his stomach had so many butterflies he thought it would fly away. Resolve was definitely going to be a problem.

# CHAPTER THREE

JACKY DOUGLAS yawned as he shuffled, still half awake, across the ranch yard toward the house. He'd gotten up early to help with chores the way he usually did when he was visiting Ryan and Dante, but even mucking out the stalls hadn't woken him up much. He nearly ran into Ryan as he approached the house.

"Why didn't you tell me you'd hired Frizz?" Jacky asked before yawning again.

"I didn't think it was a big deal," Ryan answered. "Or that the two of you had history. After the rodeo, you were pretty closed-mouthed about what happened." Ryan handed him a mug, and Jacky sighed before sipping the strong black coffee. Jacky looked away, watching one of the horses as it moved around the paddock. "I see," Ryan said. "You don't want to talk about it."

Jacky sighed. "It's not that. It's that I don't understand what happened. He was a bull rider and he was really cute. We talked at the bar and then went back to my hotel room." Jacky continued watching the horse. "That should have been it. We had a good time, and he left before morning. An easy, fun one-night stand. That's all it was."

"But it wasn't," Ryan said, and Jacky turned back toward his best friend.

"No. He was so damned innocent and open about things." Jacky sipped from the mug. "It was his first time, and he was so earnest. I know it probably sounds stupid, but I got caught up in him. There was no guile. He was so open and sweet."

Ryan chuckled softly. "So, he touched you. That's a good thing."

"I guess. But he barely looked at me at dinner last night, and afterwards he went right to his room and closed the door. When I saw him, I hoped…."

"You hoped you could pick things up right where they left off, an easy happy romp in the hay, just like the last time." Ryan slowly shook his head. "I don't know what happened a few weeks ago, but…." Ryan paused. "He's young, and while I'm just guessing here, I don't think things are as easy for him as you might have thought. I get the feeling he's still trying to figure out who he is." Ryan began to laugh, and Jacky scowled. "Not everyone bursts out of the closet the way you did."

"Uh-huh," Jacky said.

"How much do you know about him?" Ryan asked, and Jacky shrugged. Obviously, he didn't know much.

"I think if you want to get close to him, you're going to need to find out." Ryan turned and headed toward the barn. Jacky yawned again and walked toward the house. Movement at the corner of his eye caught his attention, and he followed it, watching as Frizz carried a bale of hay across one of the paddocks. Jacky leaned against the fence and watched as Frizz fed the horses and then checked their water before turning back to the barn. He waved briefly, and Jacky waved back before finishing his coffee.

Once he was done, Jacky yawned once again and went inside. He put his mug in the sink and wandered to the guest room he was using. Dante met him, grumbling under his breath as he passed.

"Morning, sunshine," Jacky teased, and Dante turned to him with a growl. "Good God, what crawled up your butt and died?"

Dante paused. "Ryan hired that kid."

"So?" Jacky said. "You'd been complaining that you needed help."

"He hired that kid as a project for me," Dante said, continuing down the hall. Jacky followed because… well, this could be interesting. "Ryan thinks I need something to occupy my time besides running this ranch and taking care of everything around here."

"And I thought I was the drama queen," Jacky quipped. Dante glared at him, and Jacky smiled. "Come on, you have to admit that was pretty queeny, and more than a little whiny."

"Ryan wants me to work with Frizz on his riding. He actually wasn't going to tell me about it until I pressed him," Dante said as he opened cupboards and banged pans loud enough to wake the dead.

"So?" Jacky said. "You saw him. Frizz is good. He needs someone to help him with the finer points and show him some style, but he has talent. You saw that; we all did." Dante growled again. "Are you all grumpy bear"—Jacky jumped back in case Dante took a swipe at him—"because you think he could be better than you? Because that's bullshit."

"Duh," Dante muttered.

"Not that he couldn't be better than you. But if you help him, then his success is yours."

"Yeah, you old grump," Ryan agreed as he walked in the room. "Stop the bear routine. Why do you think I was so angry when you went gallivanting off and told them you'd ride a few weeks ago? It wasn't that I didn't want you to ride, it's that you haven't been training and I don't want you hurt."

"Those that can, do, and those that can't, teach," Dante muttered.

"In this case, it's a world champion and expert teaching the next generation," Ryan said as he hip-bumped Dante. "Imagine what you could have done if you'd have had someone to show you the ropes instead of having to learn everything the hard way." Ryan glared at Dante, and Jacky saw the bluster go out of Dante like the air from a balloon. "You're a great rider, there's no doubt about that. Why would you want to keep what you know to yourself?"

"You're the best rider I've seen," Jacky said, and Dante turned toward him. "You have style, and even with a bull bucking and twisting, there's a graceful elegance to your riding that most people don't have. That's what everyone saw on that ride a few weeks ago."

Dante huffed. He obviously wasn't completely convinced. "Fine. I'll see what the kid can do, but don't you two mother hens expect me to coddle him."

"Heaven forbid," Ryan quipped.

"What does that mean?" Dante asked, and Ryan moved closer. He leaned close and whispered something. Jacky couldn't hear the words, but the tone held unmistakable power, and Dante shivered. Dante swallowed and nodded once. Then he went to work to make breakfast, completely dropping the subject.

"Would you tell Frizz breakfast will be ready soon?" Ryan asked him, and Jacky nodded before walking toward the front door and then out to the barn. He found Frizz in one of the stalls, taking softly to the horse inside as he worked. Jacky waited for him to come out and close the door.

"Ryan said breakfast will be ready soon," Jacky told him.

"Thanks," Frizz said before hurrying away toward the tack room. Jacky waited a few minutes, but Frizz didn't come back out, so he walked to the doorway and peered inside. Frizz stood staring out the window.

"You okay?" Jacky asked, and Frizz jumped slightly, whirling around.

"I'm fine," Frizz answered quickly and then turned away. "I'll be inside in a minute."

Jacky took a single step forward and stopped. Frizz's hands clenched and then relaxed. His posture was rigid, and he was wound tighter than a drum. He opened his mouth to say something and stopped, sighing instead before turning and leaving the room. Jacky knew when he wasn't wanted, and if Frizz wasn't interested in his attention, Jacky certainly wouldn't force anything. Without thinking about it, Jacky began walking faster and faster; the barn seemed too small and he needed to get out.

Outside by the paddock, Jacky inhaled a deep breath and blew it out before repeating it. *What in hell brought that on?* He watched the horses. He heard footsteps that paused, and then Frizz leaned against the fence next to him. He didn't talk, which Jacky found strange, but he was no longer in the mood for conversation either. All he wanted were these memories and glimpses of so long ago to fade away once again.

The horse in the paddock must have wondered what was going on, because his ears perked up and he slowly ambled over to where they stood. "That's Goofball," Jacky said as the horse got closer. He walked in front of them, brushing them and the fence, muscles rippling and shaking as he went. Then the stupid horse turned around and did the same thing to the other side. "I swear he thinks he's a cat," Jacky said flatly without taking his eyes off the chestnut gelding.

"Is his name really Goofball?" Frizz asked.

"Nah, that's just what I call him. His name's Hubble, but Goofball fits." Jacky looked at Frizz for a second. Tension rolled off him, and Jacky wondered at the source. He hadn't shifted his gaze off the horse but a second before Frizz nodded and turned toward the house. Jacky almost shivered at the ice in Frizz's behavior, wondering what he'd done, but he couldn't think of anything. Whatever was bothering Frizz wasn't Jacky's fault. Sure, the two of them had spent a fun night together. Frizz had told Jacky he'd thought about him, but almost ever since, Frizz had been distant and cold.

Jacky pushed away from the fence and walked toward the house. He smelled the food as soon as he opened the door, and his stomach rumbled loudly as he walked into the kitchen. Frizz barely looked up from his plate as Jacky sat down. Dante and Ryan joined them. "Ryan said you were a big help this morning," Dante told Frizz. "Got most of the horses fed and watered."

"Yeah. He said you did the immediate chores today and then took a day of rest, so I figured if I helped, everyone would have less to do." Frizz looked at Ryan. "Hope that was okay."

"Of course it was," Dante said. "I like a man with ambition and who'll take initiative." Jacky ate and half listened to the rest of the conversation. He was beginning to think he might as well pack up and head back to the city soon. "After breakfast I thought we could go out to the shed and see what you got," Dante said, and Jacky perked right up. "You want to come too?" Dante asked, and Jacky nodded. Then Dante turned to Ryan.

"I've got work to do before tomorrow, but I'll be out later this morning," Ryan said levelly. Dante nodded once, and Jacky looked away. He saw Frizz watching, though, with a confused look on his face. He must have known something significant was going on, but he couldn't quite figure it out. Jacky knew what it meant. He'd been around his close friends enough to know the dynamics of their relationship.

"What sort of work do you need done in the shed?" Frizz asked Dante skeptically.

"Not *work* work, riding work. You'll need some of your gear, though. I've only seen you ride once, and I really want to get a feel for what you can do." Dante reached for the plate of toast and shoved a piece in his mouth. Jacky finished eating and got up when Dante did. Frizz finished as well, and they all carried their dishes to the sink. Jacky couldn't help watching him, no matter how icy he thought Frizz was acting. He had the same build as Dante, compact and lean, but with muscular arms and legs and that red hair that seemed to want to go everywhere all at once. He remembered how soft it was and how he'd run his fingers through it while Frizz had had his lips wrapped around….

"Jacky, are you coming?" Dante asked, pulling him out of his daydream.

"Yeah," he said and quickly glanced down to make sure nothing was showing. Then he left the kitchen and followed Dante outside. Frizz caught up with them as they walked toward what had once been an old barn. Now it sported a fresh coat of paint, and over the last year had been nearly rebuilt. Dante unlocked the door and pulled it open, then turned on the lights. The bucking machine stood in the center of the room, with thick padding covering the floor almost to the walls.

Frizz whistled, and the tension that had been present all morning seemed to melt away as he stepped forward to inspect the machine. "This is cool," he said, stroking the padded "bull."

"Jacky will operate the machine for us. I'll show you how it works, and then we'll give you a chance. We're going to start at a low to medium setting and work up from there." Dante pulled on his chaps and the other equipment. "We don't really need all the safety gear since everything's padded, but I believe in training under conditions as close to real as possible." Dante turned to Frizz. "It doesn't take much to throw off your balance, so I always train with everything I'm going to wear during competition."

Frizz nodded, pulled out his gear, and began putting it on. "I understand."

"Good." Dante got into his gear and climbed on.

"First, you need to stay on the bull," Jacky said, stating the obvious

Dante looked at him, and Jacky showed him the setting. Dante nodded, and Jacky turned it on. The machine began to move. "Yes, you want to stay on the bull, but it's more than that. You need to look like you're having fun and are in command while you do it. Sure, the bull will buck, jump, and spin," Dante said as the machine went through its moves. After about thirty seconds, Dante bailed and rolled on the padding. Jacky turned off the machine and it came to a stop. "And everyone gets bucked. The thing is, while you're up there, if you want to win, you gotta make it look like it's nothing, even when you swear the damned bull is going to pull your arm out of the socket." Dante patted the back of the bull, and Frizz climbed on.

"Do I use the same grip as in competition?" Frizz asked, and Dante checked his grip and made a few modifications. "Yeah, that's better," Frizz said with a smile. Dante stepped back, and once Frizz nodded, Jacky turned on the machine.

It began to move, and Frizz held on, but Jacky could see he was fighting it. The finesse Dante had wasn't there. "Go with the movement, don't fight it," Jacky said, and Dante nodded, watching Frizz closely. Jacky saw him loosen up, and he seemed to be riding better.

"Use your free arm," Dante said. "That's better." The machine wasn't going too fast, so at a signal from Dante, Jacky sped it up. "Move with the bull and use your arm." Frizz went flying and landed almost at Jacky's feet. Jacky turned off the machine and then extended his hand to pull Frizz up. Through his glove, Jacky could feel Frizz's heat.

"That was pretty good," Jacky said.

"Thanks," Frizz whispered.

"Get back on, and this time, concentrate on your balance. That's the key to everything. Also, in the rodeo, I saw you anticipate the bull's moves. You need to work on that too. It needs to become second nature," Dante instructed, and Frizz bounded back up on the bull. Jacky started the machine and watched Frizz as he moved. Damn, he was fine, thighs straining his jeans, gripping the bull, a smile on his face. He loved what he was doing.

"Yee fucking hah!" Frizz cried as the bull went into a spin. Jacky saw Frizz anticipate it and go right with the movement. "Yeah!"

"Don't get cocky, kid," Dante said and motioned for Jacky to turn up the machine. The bull moved faster, and for a few seconds Frizz did okay, but then the bull began to get the best of him. Jacky watched as Frizz was thrown and immediately turned off the machine. Frizz groaned from the padding and then swore before getting up. Without being told, Frizz jumped back on, got his grip, and looked at Jacky.

"Let's kick some bull ass," Frizz said and then whooped as Jacky turned on the machine. Again and again, Frizz was thrown, but each time he stayed on a bit longer.

"That's enough," Dante pronounced after a while. "You need to rest a little. There's water in the fridge over there. Grab a couple and drink. We're going to give Jacky here a shot."

For him, it was just fun. He set the machine where he wanted it and climbed on the bull. He didn't go too fast, but when Dante started the machine, he whooped and grinned like he was in the main ring at the finals. He didn't last too long, but the ride was fun.

Then Dante took a turn, and Frizz stood next to him as Jacky set the machine on maximum. He signaled, and Jacky turned on the machine. Jacky glanced at Frizz, who sat enthralled as Dante twisted and moved with the machine. It was like poetry in motion. Jacky watched Frizz watching Dante. He felt a bit like he was in a three-way for a second, and then Frizz glanced at him and smiled.

He was lost for a split second. Then he turned in time to see Dante tumble off the bull. Jacky stopped the machine and hurried over to where Dante lay on the padding. "Are you okay?"

"I'm fine," Dante said, laughing. Then he pulled Jacky closer. "If you two spent any more time screwing each other with your eyes, you could make it a full-time job." Dante let him go and laughed again as he got up. "I think that's enough for the day." Dante continued chuckling until the door opened and Ryan stepped inside.

The temperature seemed to jump in an instant. Dante stared at Ryan, and he stared back, electric current zinging between them. Dante stood stock-still, and Ryan stalked toward him without saying a word. Their gazes locked, and Jacky realized he and Frizz no longer existed to either of them. Dante and Ryan only had eyes for each other right now, and sexual energy crackled in the air. Jacky took Frizz's arm and tilted his head toward the door. Then he almost pulled the other man out of the barn and closed the door behind them.

"What was all that about?" Frizz whispered, turning around to stare at the door as if it held the answer he was looking for. He shivered slightly, and Jacky released his arm.

"That was all-consuming passion," Jacky explained. "Those two were meant for each other like no two other people I've ever met. They're the other half of each other. Dante can cook; Ryan can't. Ryan is a genius with money; Dante is amazing with the animals and running the ranch. What Dante needs, Ryan can give, and the other way around." Jacky pointed toward the house, and they headed that way.

"I thought the ranch was Dante's," Frizz said.

"Technically it's from his family, but they consider everything they have as theirs," Jacky explained and watched confusion flow across Frizz's expression. "What's got you so flustered?"

"How can that be?" Frizz stopped walking and turned to him. "You talk like they're married or something," he said, his confusion increasing, and Jacky chuckled even as he tried to look at things the way Frizz might have seen them.

"Why wouldn't they be? They've been together for a few years now, and they might get married if they could." Jacky continued walking toward the house, and Frizz hurried to catch up.

"Why? It's just sex," Frizz said, and Jacky whirled around.

"Is that what you think? That being gay is just about sex?" Jacky realized he was talking louder than necessary, looked to see if any of the other hands were around, and saw some of the other men heading out of the barn toward one of the trucks. Jacky quieted himself and strode toward the house. He didn't look to see if Frizz was following. Inside, he sighed and sat in the living room. A minute later Frizz sat down near him, but didn't say anything.

"I'm sorry," Frizz said, and Jacky turned toward him. "I thought…."

"No," Jacky said. "I know what you thought, and being gay is about a lot more than just sex. Having sex or wanting to have sex with another man does not make you gay. Sex is sex. What makes you gay is who you fall in love with. If a man can fall in love with another man, then he's gay. If a man has sex with other men and falls in love with women, then he's bisexual, metrosexual, or maybe just confused." Jacky chuckled at his intended joke, but Frizz just stared back at him and shook his head.

"I don't get the joke," Frizz said.

"It was a bad one. The thing is, Dante and Ryan love each other. They'd do anything for each other. If someone were to hurt Dante, they'd have to deal with Ryan too."

"But how is that possible? I was always taught that relations between two men were sinful, and that it was just a weakness that had to be overcome," Frizz said. "You need to control your base desires, so you can marry and have children."

"Is that what you really think?" Jacky asked, and Frizz shrugged. Jacky stood up and moved closer to him. He locked gazes with Frizz, reached out, and lightly cupped his cheeks in his hands. Then Jacky leaned closer and kissed him. Their lips touched, and Jacky deepened the kiss just a little. Frizz moaned softly and then pulled away. "Is that what you still think?"

Frizz shrugged again, so Jacky kissed him again. This time he added more intensity. Little ripples of energy shot up Jacky's spine and his head throbbed slightly. Frizz's unique, rich flavor burst on his tongue when he tickled Frizz's lips. He wanted to press Frizz back and take control, maybe strip the other man of his clothes and remind him of the passion they'd shared in the hotel room a few weeks earlier. But he pulled back, even as Frizz whimpered.

Frizz swallowed hard, and Jacky moved back and then sat back in his chair. "You can't tell me you didn't feel that," Jacky said, and Frizz nodded slowly. "There's more to it than just sex. I've kissed men before, and I've spent the night with them. But I never felt the zing of energy with any of them that I feel with you." Jacky leaned forward. "And if you think the night we had in the hotel was just sex, then you're crazy. There was something else there. I don't know how to describe it to you other than to say that most of the time sex is nice, but it doesn't make you black out from sheer bliss." Jacky released a deep breath as he remembered their night together.

"It isn't always like this?" Frizz asked.

Jacky shook his head. "No." He stood up, left the room, and went to the guest room. He needed to get ready to go back to the city. He put his suitcase on the neatly made bed and opened it. He needed to work in the morning, and there wasn't any more he could say to Frizz. He was so young and innocent. He didn't understand anything, and Jacky had no doubt Frizz wasn't out to anyone other than the few people on the ranch. Yes, he thought they might have the chance at something special, but he wasn't sure Frizz was ready for anything like that, or if he wanted to be involved with someone so deeply in the closet.

"So what's it really like, then?" Frizz asked, and Jacky turned around to find him standing in the doorway.

"I don't know," Jacky said. "What's it like to be in any other relationship? Because that's what it is. Lots of people want to think that being gay is just sex, because then it's easy for them to put us in whatever box they want. They did it to you. You've heard all your life that being gay is wrong," Jacky said, and Frizz nodded. "I heard the same thing, and I believed it too. Only it was much worse, because I was never a kid who could hide very well. That made me a target for most of my teenage years. It wasn't until I got to college and found people who were open-minded enough to care about me regardless, and I met other people like me. Before that, I sometimes thought I was the only person in the world like this."

"I thought that too," Frizz said. "Then I met you and I wasn't alone anymore. But what we did is still wrong. The Bible says so. I've heard it since I was a kid." Frizz turned away from the door.

"Did you ever think that what you'd been taught might be wrong?" Jacky asked as hope bloomed. If Frizz was asking questions, then there might be a chance.

Frizz stopped. "I have to resist my urges."

"Is that what you think?" Jacky asked. "I was raised in the same kind of Christian home as you. I was taught to push aside what I wanted, and if I immersed myself in the Bible and what was right, then I could lead a normal life. My stepfather told me that all the time. But you see, my mother didn't buy it, not after a while."

"She accepted you?" Frizz asked. "Mine will never accept me. Not matter what, that I can count on. I know what you said about the fear being worse than the reality, but in my case that's not true. You don't know my family." Frizz was pained; that was obvious. "If I don't behave and act like I should, they'll fire me as their son." The strange wording caught Jacky's attention. "My dad made that pretty clear before I left." Frizz left the doorway, and Jacky heard his footsteps retreat down the hall.

Jacky looked at his suitcase. He really should pack his things and say good-bye to Dante and Ryan when they resurfaced, then head back to the city and forget all about Frizz and his hang-ups. He'd met tons of men like this before, and it always ended badly. In college, there'd been Juan, who was wonderful, and Jacky had fallen in love with him, completely head over heels. But Juan couldn't get past all the crap his family and church had pounded into his head. He and Juan had dated for six months, and then Juan had dumped him to go out with a woman. He'd actually married her. Jacky swallowed hard as he thought about it. "Just get out of here and let the closet-case kid do whatever he wants," Jacky muttered under his breath. He'd had enough heartbreak at the hands of closet cases in his life, and he certainly didn't need to ask for more.

He sighed and packed his things before closing the suitcase. Then he left the room and wandered down the hall to the living room, where he found Frizz sitting on the sofa, staring at a blank television screen. "You can turn on the television if you want," Jacky said. Frizz barely seemed to hear him. Jacky stepped around the sofa and sat down. "Do you want to talk about it?" Frizz shrugged, and Jacky reached for the remote. He found an episode of *Castle* and settled in to watch.

"Do you know who my parents are?" Frizz asked, and Jacky turned down the volume. "My name is Simon Frizzell. That's why I go by Frizz at the rodeos. I let people think it's because of my hair, but it's not."

"Okay," Jacky said.

"My folks own Frizzell's Family Bookstores," Frizz said, turning away from the screen. "A week ago, my dad fired one of his managers for being gay. Of course, he found another reason to let him go, but he wouldn't have been looking if the guy hadn't been gay. I know if they find out, my dad will fire me too. See, it doesn't matter what I want or how I feel—I have to be normal. I can't be this way, not in my family."

Jacky thought Frizz was going to cry for a few seconds. It appeared to him as though Frizz's heart was breaking, but then his expression hardened and he turned back to the television.

"You know that being true to yourself is just as important as what your family wants," Jacky said.

Frizz shook his head. "No, it isn't. If I'm gay, then my folks will hate me and they'll kick me out of the family. I'll never see any of my brothers and sisters again." Frizz paused. "I'll lose everything."

Jacky had no idea what to say to him. He'd had to come to the realization of who he was and that he was going to live his life in the open, and he'd done it quite a while ago. Jacky stared at the screen and said nothing. Everything inside him said to run. That this wasn't worth it, and he was going to end up with a broken heart when Frizz left him for some girl. They'd end up getting married and live unhappily ever after, but it would be what Frizz's family wanted. So that was all that was going to matter as long as Frizz was hiding and not willing to be true to himself. What was worse was there was nothing Jacky could do about it.

They sat quietly, watching the program. As it was ending, Ryan and Dante came in the house. Dante seemed exceptionally relaxed. Even Frizz seemed to notice.

"You know, you won't lose everything," Jacky finally said. "Because you'll have accepted who you are." Jacky knew that was a huge step for anyone and required a giant leap of faith. "There will be people who will hate you and people who will stand by you no matter what."

"But my parents," Frizz whispered. "How can I take the chance?"

"How can you not find out who you are? I bet your parents didn't raise you to lie to yourself, and that's what you're doing by denying who you are," Jacky said in a whisper. He figured it would make Frizz more comfortable.

"I don't know," Frizz answered. "I'm really confused right now."

Jacky lightly patted Frizz's knee. "I understand. We all go through that as we begin to realize we're different. Being different is okay, you know." Jacky stood up. "You need to give yourself a little time to think things over, and this is a good place to do it. It's safe. No one here is going to judge you or think badly of you because you're gay." Jacky turned to leave the room.

"You're leaving?"

"Yes. I need to get back to the city. I was only visiting for the weekend."

"Right, I remember Ryan saying you lived in Houston."

"Ryan's my best friend, though, so I see them quite a bit. Sometimes it's nice to be able to get away from the noise and bustle of the city to a place where it's quiet."

"And Jacky has a real thing for cowboys," Ryan teased as he came into the room. "He can't seem to stay away. We'll have lunch before you go," Ryan told him with a friendly pat on the shoulder, and then he headed for the kitchen.

"You aren't cooking, are you?" Jacky asked as a dab of fear shot through him. The last time Ryan had tried to cook, they'd all spent the evening in mortal fear of food poisoning. It hadn't materialized, but they'd all learned a lesson: for the sake of their stomachs and taste buds, they didn't let Ryan cook.

"He's not cooking," Dante said with a smile as he came in the room. "We're having sandwiches." Dante pulled Ryan close, and the two of them shared a brief moment. Jacky turned away. He loved how they were so close they could communicate with each other without words, but it made him jealous as well. That was what he wanted, but knew he'd never be able to find.

"I'll help," Frizz said and got up from the sofa. He followed Ryan into the kitchen. Jacky couldn't help following him with his eyes, watching that firm cowboy butt swing back and forth in those jeans.

"You've got it bad, don't you?" Dante asked once the others were gone.

Jacky rolled his eyes. "I know, and it's so stupid. He's young, in the closet, and he's still trying to figure out who he is. The last time I was with a guy like him, it wasn't pretty at all, and I'm not sure I can go through all that again." He looked at Dante earnestly, hoping for some advice. Instead, Dante chuckled and covered his mouth before breaking into full-scale laughter.

"Forget it, Jacky. You're already so far gone you can barely stand it. I saw the way you watched him when we were working out earlier. You couldn't take your eyes off him, and your tongue practically hung out of your mouth the entire time."

"It did not," Jacky argued lamely.

"Sure, it did," Dante countered. "You can't fight what your heart wants. I tried that with Ryan and it didn't work."

"Well, we aren't you and Ryan, that's for sure," Jacky said. "No, I think Frizz and I are probably meant to have the one time we had together. Anything else is wishful thinking on my part." Jacky heard them moving in the kitchen and stood up. After turning off the television, he and Dante joined the others. Ryan and Dante kept stealing glances at each other and sharing little smiles that were so insipidly sweet Jacky had to look away or he was going to scream with jealousy.

Jacky busied himself making his sandwich and passing the fixings to others. He pointedly tried not to look at Frizz, because as much as he wanted to think Dante was full of shit, he *had* been watching Frizz the entire time. Yes, Frizz hadn't moved the way Dante had, but that hadn't mattered. He loved the way Frizz had gripped the bull with his legs and the way he moved his hips to keep his balance. Jacky pulled his mind away from those images and concentrated on making his lunch.

"I have a client meeting first thing in the morning," Ryan said to Dante, who nodded.

"How far of a drive do you have?" Frizz asked Ryan.

"It's about an hour, to the northern edge of Houston," Ryan answered. "Thankfully, that's where my office is, so I don't have to drive through the city every day."

"You don't work here?" Frizz asked with surprise.

"Some days I work out of the office here. A couple days a week, I go into the office in the city, and other days I'm out visiting clients. Those are the longest days, because I often end up traveling all over. But it's part of being a money manager. You go to your clients." Ryan took a bite of his sandwich. "Jacky lives near where I used to."

Jacky nodded but didn't say anything.

"I was checking, and there's a rodeo in a few weeks. It's up near Beaumont. They're still looking for entrants." Ryan glanced at Dante, and then they both looked at Frizz. "Did you want to enter?"

"It's a good one," Dante said. "You'd have to practice a lot, but you could be ready, with hard work." Frizz nodded, and then Dante turned to Jacky. "We'll get you a ticket if you want to come."

Jacky glanced at Frizz and then back at Dante. "I'll have to let you know," he said and added a smile. Dante seemed a little surprised, but thankfully said nothing. Jacky continued eating and deliberately went quiet. He wasn't really in the mood to talk. He needed to leave, get home, and have some time to think. Frizz had him flustered and damned confused. Jacky always thought he'd known what he wanted in a man—a strong cowboy who didn't give a damn about what the rest of the world thought about anything. That definitely wasn't Frizz. Sure, he had the cowboy part down, but he was young, maybe too young, and he certainly cared what the world thought about him. Jacky wasn't sure about the strong part yet either. But one thing was undeniable—he was most definitely attracted to Frizz. His eyes and the way he moved would be hard for Jacky to forget, no matter how much he wanted to.

Jacky finished eating and got up from the table. He placed his dishes in the sink and then sat back down. He joined the conversation, but as soon as they others were finished, he went to the guest room to make sure he'd left everything the way he'd found it. Then he checked that he hadn't left anything behind before grabbing his suitcase. He found the others in the living room and hugged Ryan and Dante good-bye. Then he said good-bye to Frizz and headed out to his car. He threw his suitcase in the trunk and closed the lid before getting in the car. As soon as he'd pulled the door closed and started the engine, he released a deep breath.

He always came to the ranch to chill and spend time with his friends, but this weekend had not been relaxing in the least. He'd ridden a roller coaster finishing in a death spiral that had finally come to an end, and Jacky was more than ready to get off. He put the car in gear, turned it around, and headed down the drive to the road.

A little over an hour later, Jacky pulled into his parking space in his condo complex and turned off the engine. He'd spent the entire drive thinking about Frizz, and it drove him crazy. He needed to put him out of his mind and let him go. That was all there was to it. They'd had a night together, that was all. He needed to walk away and let Frizz figure things out for himself. Jacky knew he should simply wish him well and let that be the end of it.

He got out of the car and opened the truck, resolved on his course of action. He was simply going to stay away from the ranch for a while and let this infatuation pass. With that settled, he grabbed his suitcase, closed the trunk, and strode toward the condo door.

As the days went by, Jacky's resolve held. He spent the next weekend at a club, dancing and having the time of his life with a room full of men. Everything was fine until a huge stud in tight jeans, a western shirt, and a cowboy hat walked up to him, looked him in the eye, and kissed him right then and there. Jacky was in heaven until the guy pulled back and led Jacky toward one of the tables. For a second Jacky thought he'd hit the jackpot, exactly what he'd wanted: a hot, in-charge cowboy. But once they sat down, he saw the shadow of bronzer on the guy's shirt, and as he looked closer, he definitely noticed the even tan and moisturized skin. "Let's have a beer and see about starting a little rodeo of our own," the cowboy said, and Jacky had to stop himself from laughing. "Is everything all right?" the man asked, but then, apparently sensing rejection, he got up, stepped away from the table, and disappeared into the crowd of men.

"What happened?" Jacky's friend Claude asked as he approached the table. Jacky could hardly hear him over the beat of the music, and Claude had to shout his question again. "I would have thought he'd have been just your thing." Claude slid into the other chair, and Jacky could hear him better.

"He was so fake," Jacky answered, "and to top it off, he had the voice of a teenage girl." Jacky watched the crowd and couldn't help chuckling again. "Talk about see Tarzan, hear Jane."

"Oh, God, I hate that. I went out with this guy once. He was a bodybuilder, legs like tree trunks and arms to bend steel, but as soon as he opened his mouth, he sounded like my Aunt Helen." Claude snickered, and then they both let go and had a good laugh.

"What did you do?" Jacky asked once he caught his breath,

"I took him home. He was one hell of a lay, although when he screamed, I kept expecting the windows to shatter." They both began laughing again. "We ended up dating for two months, until my eardrums couldn't take it any longer." Claude stuck his fingers in his ears, and they laughed again. "What's been up with you?" Claude asked once they'd settled down again.

Jacky shrugged and turned to glance over the crowd.

"You've had guys interested all night. What gives?" Claude pressed, and Jacky shook his head. "Then let's go. You're obviously not up for this." Claude slipped out of the booth, and Jacky followed, weaving through the crowd to the exit. He and Claude had been friends forever, and Jacky had wondered a few times why they'd never gotten together, but it had just never happened. Now they were great friends, and he wouldn't change that for the world.

"Let's go back to my place," Jacky offered. Since they'd been drinking, he found a taxi and gave the driver the address. It didn't take long before they pulled through the gate and into the complex. At his building, Jacky paid the driver, and they got out. Claude had had more to drink than Jacky, and he stumbled a little before they made it inside. Jacky threw his keys in the bowl and shut the door. Claude went inside and collapsed on the sofa.

"So," Claude began, speaking rather loudly. "What's been up with you lately?" he asked, and Jacky went into the kitchen to brew a pot of coffee. "We go out, and a hunk of the first order is interested. Sure, he sounded like Tinker Bell, but he was as big as a house and a cowboy to boot." Claude sprawled out on the sofa as Jacky came in the room and sat in his favorite chair.

"You're drunk," Jacky said.

Claude straightened up. "No, I'm not. I'm just really mellow." Claude wasn't much bigger than Jacky, but he was cute in a boyish sort of way. Both of them were in their late twenties, but Claude still got carded when they went to clubs, and most people pegged him for barely legal. Jacky had always figured it was the floppy, poodleish way he wore his blond hair, or his amazing blue eyes, but it was more than that. He looked young, and the boys loved him for it. "So give me the dirt. What's got you off your feed?"

The condo filled with the scent of brewing coffee. Jacky got up and poured two mugs. When he returned, he handed one to Claude before sitting back in his chair. He glanced at the clock—it wasn't even midnight yet, and he was already home. That was pathetic for a Saturday night at the clubs. "A couple of weeks ago I went to the rodeo and met this guy. He's a bull rider, and we spent the night together."

Claude perked up and sipped from his mug. "And you're still thinking about him. That must have been some night."

"It was, but because… it was his first time." Jacky took a sip of coffee to hide his smile. "It was really special. Anyway," he continued, pulling himself out of the memory, "I saw him again last weekend at Dante and Ryan's. They've hired him on, and Dante is showing him the finer points of riding bulls."

"Okay, so this sounds good. You saw him again, there was the same spark…." Claude made a "go on" gesture with his fingers. "So what happened?"

"Nothing. He's a nice guy, and when I'm around him I can't take my eyes off him."

"So…."

"He's too young and he's still trying to figure out what he wants. I've been through all that, God knows…." Jacky shifted in the chair. "For the past week I've tried to put him out of my mind, and it was working until the fake cowboy opened his mouth." Frizz had this melted-butter voice that wrapped around him and….

"So you've spent all week trying to forget this closet case, and you passed up the fake cowboy because you can't stop thinking about him?" Claude asked, sipping his coffee. "You got it bad."

"A lot of good it's going to do me. Frizz—that's the closet case, as you put it—is riding in a rodeo next weekend. Dante and Ryan are going, and they asked if I wanted to go along."

"What did you say?"

"That I'd have to let them know. I'd love to go to the rodeo with them, but I think I should stay away and let everything sort of die down."

"I think that's a good idea," Claude said. "Where's this rodeo?"

"In Beaumont. Why?"

Claude set his mug on the coffee table. "I'd love to go to the rodeo. Do you think you could call Dante and Ryan and ask if I could go along? I'd like to see this guy who has you all tied up in knots."

"Go ahead," Jacky said, handing Claude his phone.

"So you wouldn't mind if I went to the rodeo and took Frizz out for a drink afterwards? If he wins, I could take him some place special to celebrate." Claude shook his head slightly, curly bangs falling in his eyes. Jacky had seen that move more times than he could count, and it was always great for getting guys' attention. Heat rose in Jacky's face until he could feel it in his ears. "*Really* celebrate, if you know what I mean."

Before he could stop himself, Jacky was out of the chair and across the room. He jumped on top of Claude and held him down on the sofa. His heart pounding, face on fire, Jacky glared at Claude. "He's a good guy and doesn't deserve that," he spat. His anger lasted until he saw Claude smile. "You bastard," Jacky said and stepped off the sofa.

"You're so damned easy to read it's pathetic. You really like this guy, and he's got you so tied in knots you don't know which way to turn." Claude laughed harder. "If you want to know what I think, I say go to that damned rodeo. You said the kid needs to figure things out, but I think it's you who needs to get things straightened out in his head."

"He's still in the closet," Jacky said.

"So give him something to compare the closet to," Claude quipped.

"Have you ever gotten your heart broken by someone in the closet?"

"Blah, blah, blah," Claude said. "So Juan dumped you for a chick. I saw him out trolling for what he really wanted last month, and the little woman was staying at home. I wasn't sure it was him at first—he's not aged well. Remember when we saw him at the mall a few years ago? Well, he's ballooned since then."

"So?" Jacky whined.

"So, you're letting a fat closet case get in the way of you and this bull rider. If I could show you a picture, you'd shudder and be so glad you weren't curled up to that each and every night." Claude shivered for dramatic effect, and Jacky smiled. He had to leave it to Claude—he knew how to make him feel better. "So get over it."

"Okay," Jacky said. "I'll go to the rodeo and see what happens."

Claude rolled his eyes. "Is Frizz just as smitten with you as you are with him?" Jacky shrugged. "Come on, you've been around long enough to know if a guy is attracted to you."

"I think he is, yes," Jacky answered. "But he's scared."

"Can you blame him? Remember how scared and dumb we were at his age?" Claude asked, and Jacky nodded, wondering where Claude was going with this, because it didn't sound like he was making his case. "But can you also remember what it felt like to be in love? How we would have given anything for that feeling? Sure, we screwed everything in sight, but we also wished each one-night stand would turn into the love of our lives. Remember how your heart pounded with hope until he got up and left?"

"Yeah, I remember," Jacky said.

"You have that chance," Claude told him. "This kid obviously isn't into the one-night stand thing, so do you think he might be into you? And that he's having a hard time dealing? From what you said, he was fed a lot of crap for a long time, and no one gets over that all at once. I sure as hell wish I'd had someone help me wade through the seven levels of hell my father the reverend built up for me. He and I haven't said a word to one another since I came out of the closet, other than things that should never pass the lips of a man of the cloth."

Jacky shifted and sat next to Claude. He figured from here on out, the conversation was probably going to take a turn down Maudlin Lane. It usually did when Claude got on the subject of his father. "It's okay. I won't let Frizz go through what your folks put you through."

"No one should be thrown out of their home for being who they are. Not even if their father catches them trying on his mother's clothes," Claude said. The alcohol must have really hit him, because the sobriety and lucidity he'd displayed since arriving began to slip away. "Just because I looked better in them than she did…." Claude giggled and then broke down into laughter that morphed into tears. It was an old hurt that Claude had never gotten over. Jacky held him and slowly rocked back and forth until Claude began to fall asleep. Then Jacky gently laid him down on the sofa and got a blanket and pillow. Once he had Claude settled, Jacky put the coffee mugs in the kitchen and got ready for bed.

# CHAPTER FOUR

SIMON paced the area outside the ring, waiting for his turn. This was his first ride, and he wanted it to go well. He had another tomorrow in the final round of competition. "You're going to be fine," Dante said, and Simon turned around. "You need to calm your nerves and get in a place where you're ready to ride." Simon took a deep breath and blew it out, but it didn't help. "You need to control your thoughts and take yourself to a place where you're calm and in control."

"I don't have a place like that," Simon said.

"Then you need to find one, develop one," Dante said.

Simon could feel the frustration pouring off himself and he wasn't sure what to do. "Think of how you felt yesterday when you and I were out for a ride," Jacky said from where he stood next to Dante. "Or think of the last time you were on the mechanical bull. How in control you were. How that thing could throw everything at you and you knew what it was going to do."

"Yeah," Simon said, his stomach jumping from nerves.

"So go there. Remember how that felt," Jacky told him. "You were in control. Block out everything else—the crowd, the clowns, all of us. Just concentrate on you and the bull. Nothing else matters." Jacky touched his shoulder, and Simon sat on the bench and closed his eyes. A cry went up from the crowd outside where he waited. He could hear the announcer, but now everything sounded muffled. Simon closed his eyes and let everything fade away.

"I'm okay," he mumbled over and over again. His heart slowed and he felt less like he was going to throw up. He breathed through his mouth and refused to think about the competition.

"Okay," Jacky said, and Simon stood up. He got his gear and walked through the break in the stands to the bull chute. He turned and waved to the crowd but didn't really see them. Then he got into position and made sure his bull rope was just right. Once he was sure everything was okay, he climbed on and got settled before signaling he was ready.

The chute opened, and the bull jumped out into the ring. All the training he'd done and everything Dante had told him slipped from his mind, and he reacted on sheer instinct. He felt the power bursting from beneath him and he held on, moving with the bull and even anticipating his next move. When the buzzer sounded, Simon bailed off and raced for the rail. He climbed over and out of danger before pulling off his helmet and waving it for the crowd.

"You did great!" Jacky stood near the rail.

Simon jumped down and left the arena, still waving his hat. He could hardly believe that ride, and his feet barely touched the ground.

As soon as he was out of sight of the crowd, Simon let out a whoop and punched the air in excitement. "That felt so dang good," he told the small group that surrounded him. "I could just feel it, like everything was there. A few times I thought I was done, but the focus you taught me helped me hang in for those few critical seconds."

"I saw," Dante said with a smile that Simon hoped included a touch of pride. "You're really improving and your confidence is great. But," Dante said, his expression becoming serious, "everyone gets bucked at some point. No one rides every bull every time, and there will be one that turns out to be your nemesis. I had one for a while." Simon nodded, trying to take in what Dante was saying, but he was too damned excited.

"Do you want to watch for a while?" Jacky asked. "We could go back to the trailer if you want a few minutes to get your thoughts together." The crowd cheered.

"The score for Simon the Frizz is 90.12. The best ride so far." He rushed back into the arena and waved his hat at the crowd, who cheered once again. This was totally awesome. Simon was on cloud nine as he left the arena.

"Okay, hotshot, let's get you away from here before your head explodes," Dante said. They left the arena area and walked to the edge of the rodeo grounds to where the trailer was parked. They'd come in the trailer Dante had used the last few years he was on the road. It had definitely seen a lot of miles, but inside it was comfortable enough for the four of them. Simon slid onto one of the bench seats at the fold-down table. He noticed as Jacky paused for a second and then sat down next to him.

Dante opened the refrigerator and pulled out bottles of water, then put them on the table. Simon grabbed one and chugged down the contents, still smiling excitedly.

"Ryan and I are going to wander around. I'm going to talk to some old friends," Dante said before grabbing two bottles of water. Then he pushed open the trailer door and they left, leaving Simon alone with Jacky. Even after drinking the entire bottle of water, his mouth was still dry. "I was surprised that you came," Simon said.

"I like rodeo, and they invited me," Jacky said as he stared at the water bottle in his hands. "I almost didn't come."

"Because you're mad at me," Simon said.

Jacky shifted on the seat before getting up and moving to the other side. "I'm not mad at you." He took a deep breath. "I like you, and that's the problem. You aren't interested in me the way I'm interested in you, and I thought some distance would give me a little perspective. It didn't." Jacky chuckled, but there was no joy in it.

Simon got up for another bottle of water and cracked it open before sitting back down. "It isn't that I'm not interested in you. It's that I can't… I shouldn't."

"I know how you feel, and that's part of why I've stayed away. If I were around a lot, you'd start to feel uncomfortable, and…." Jacky trailed off, and Simon leaned forward.

"Just say what you want to say."

"Look, we're guys. In a moment of weakness, we'd probably end up together at some point. We might do things like we did in the hotel when we first met." Jacky reached across the table and lightly touched Simon's cheek. Simon was torn between leaning into the touch, because he wanted it so badly, and pulling away. Instead he sat stock-still. "The thing is, you'd feel guilty about what you'd done, and I don't want that." Jacky shrugged. "I've had more than my share of guilt and recrimination in my life. And I won't be the source of it for someone else."

"It just goes against everything I was taught," Simon said as his stomach churned. Being this close to Jacky, he wanted to stay in control, but his body betrayed him. Simon shifted to make things more comfortable. "Ryan and I have talked a few times."

"He's a really great guy," Jacky told him.

"He is, and he's tried to answer my questions." One evening, when Dante was out sitting with one of the horses, Simon had worked up the nerve to talk to Ryan about being gay. It hadn't been easy, but he'd finally found the guts to satisfy his curiosity. Ryan had kindly and patiently answered all his questions, including the biblical and religious ones. Jacky nodded but didn't say anything, and Simon figured he might as well go for broke. "I think I'm starting to understand who I am."

"It's not a quick process. We all have to dig deep and realize we are who we are and that some of the stuff we were taught is crap. Some people never do, and they're often the ones who end up hurting themselves or others."

"Ryan said that too," Simon told Jacky. "I think the best thing he told me was to follow my heart. Regardless of what I'd been taught or what people told me, my heart would never steer me wrong." Simon took a deep breath and stood up. He walked around to the other side of the table and sat down next to Jacky. Then he turned toward him.

"What is your heart telling you now?" Jacky asked, and rather than answer, Simon leaned in and kissed him. It wasn't particularly elegant or smooth, but it was what he felt. Jacky lightly cupped his cheeks and kissed him back. Simon moaned softly and closed his eyes as warmth spread through him. Simon moved closer, and Jacky released his cheeks and pulled him in, leaning back until Simon was practically on top of him. Jacky's warmth came through his clothes, and Simon bucked a few times, gasping at the zing of pleasure that shot through him. Jacky kissed him hard, and Simon gasped, gulping air before returning the kiss. "Jesus," Jacky gasped when the kiss broke, and Simon nodded. His eyes widened when Jacky slid his hand down his back, cupping his butt through his jeans.

"Yeah," Simon gasped, and Jacky kissed him again.

His mind swam and he forgot where he was and everything else he'd been worried about. Jacky increased the pressure on his butt, pressing them closer together. Simon whined as his dick throbbed in his jeans. He was so danged close—just a little more friction and he'd tumble over the edge.

A knock sounded on the door, and Simon jumped back, hitting his head on one of the overhead cupboards. He rubbed it and sat back down on the other side of the table, his face heating from embarrassment. Then the door opened and Ryan came inside. "There's a chili cook-off starting in a little while. Dante's already in line, and he asked me to come get you two." He pulled the door closed to keep the cooler air inside. "What happened to you?" Ryan asked, and Simon colored, unable to meet his eyes.

"I hit my head on the cupboard," he answered softly, and Ryan turned around, looking at where Simon had hit his head.

"I see," Ryan said, but thankfully he didn't push further, for which Simon was eternally grateful. He was already about as red as he could get, and if he got any more embarrassed, his head was likely to explode.

"Let's go get something to eat," Jacky said, getting up. Simon did the same and followed the others out of the trailer. His head still ached, but he stopped himself from rubbing it. Ryan locked the door and then strode across the rodeo grounds to the covered pavilions, where a thick crowd had gathered.

"This is what I love about rodeo," Dante said as he looked around. "Regular folks having a real good time." A band began playing and familiar Texas country music filled the air, joining the decadent scent of chili spices, tomatoes, and God knew what else. "It sounds and smells like home."

"Amen to that," one of the huge cowboys ahead of them in line said and then paused. "You're Dante Rivers, aren't you? I saw you win the world championship. Whooee, you gave that crowd something to remember."

"I'm not sure if that's a good thing or not," Dante quipped, and Simon darted his gaze between the two men.

"It's what happens in the arena that counts—everything else is folks wagging their tongues." He held out his hand, and Dante shook it. "Carver O'Day. It's a pleasure to meet you." The line began to move, and Carver turned back around and rejoined his group.

There were all kinds of chili, and Simon separated from the group to get a bowl of something called Hawaiian chili. He figured it was chili with pineapple or something, and the hint of sweetness smelled wonderful. He paid and got his plate and bowl before looking around to see where the others were.

"Come sit with us," one of the bull riders said as he sidled up next to him. Simon recognized some of the bronc busters as well.

"Thanks, but I'm looking for my friends," Simon said and craned his neck to see where the others had gotten to.

"I'm Hank."

"Frizz," he said automatically.

"You should sit with the real men. If you hang out with them too much, people will start to talk." He led the way to a table off to the side, and Simon followed. "You shouldn't be sitting with the fruits." He continued on, and Simon followed, hoping he saw the others along the way. At the table, Hank set down his bowl, and the others sat as well. "Guys, this is Frizz. I rescued him from the gang of fruits."

"Excuse me," Simon said. "But I was with Dante Rivers, former world-champion bull rider."

"The head fruit," one of the other men said, and the group laughed.

"The 'head fruit,' as you call him, is the owner of the ranch where I work, and he's also the guy who's been gracious enough to take his time to help me train." Simon turned to leave.

"Like I said, you need to be careful who you hang with," Hank called, and Simon stopped and turned around.

"You know, you're right. See, if I sit here, people might mistake me for a moron." Simon turned and walked through the crowd. He spotted Ryan and made a beeline for the table. Simon put down his bowl and sat next to Jacky. He glanced out of the corner of his eye and saw the others watching him. He had no doubt he'd just made some enemies, but talk like that was….

"We thought we lost you," Jacky said with a tiny smile. "I saw you moving to sit with the other riders. It's okay if you want to eat with them." Jacky turned, and Simon followed his gaze.

"You mean eat with the rocket scientists? No thanks," Simon said, then tasted the chili. It was spicy, but the sweetness cut it, and he hummed softly while taking another spoonful.

Dante passed him a beer. "You need to be careful," he said. "There are a lot of great rodeo people, but cowboys can be intolerant assholes sometimes." Dante turned to Ryan, and his partner moved a little closer. "Have a beer or two, but no more. These are great gatherings, but watch what you drink and the people around you." Dante leaned over the table. "Don't go wandering around late at night, especially alone. Good people sometimes have too much to drink, and old prejudices die hard. I don't want anyone to end up as a target."

Simon instantly knew he should have simply excused himself and left rather than opening his big mouth. But it was too late now. He thought about turning around to see what the riders were doing, but decided not to. No need to antagonize anyone further. They talked the finer points of chili and ate until they were ready to burst.

"Was everything good?" Carver asked as he walked up to the table, and Dante motioned him to a seat. "Don't mean to interrupt, but it's not every day a world champion just walks up behind you."

"I'm just a rancher now," Dante said. "Got a family spread north of Houston. Not real big, but it's home. We raise cattle with some horses."

"Me too," Carver said. "Got ten thousand head of longhorns just east of here." He looked at all of them, and Dante made introductions. They shook hands, and Carver looked like he was settling in.

"You from around here?" Carver asked him, and Simon shook his head.

"Oklahoma. My folks have horses and such. I wanted to ride bulls, and I was lucky enough to have met Dante at my last rodeo."

"You had a good ride today," Carver said. "Been riding long?"

"Whenever I could over the past few years. There aren't many bulls near home, so I had to travel before I got the job here." Something about the way Carver looked at him made Simon wonder if something was going on, or worse, if he recognized him from somewhere. It wasn't likely, but….

"I swear I know you from somewhere, but I haven't been to Oklahoma lately. It was good to see you ride, and I hope you do as well tomorrow, young fella." Carver stood back up. "Don't mean to interrupt your meal, but wanted to say hello and take a second to jaw with a rodeo legend." Carver tipped his hat and then moved away from the table.

"I'm going for more," Dante said, and he stood up. Ryan did as well, leaving Simon and Jacky alone.

"Do you want to tell me what happened with those guys? You've looked sort of freaked since you sat down," Jacky whispered. "I can imagine it wasn't particularly flattering."

Simon nodded and tilted his hat upward slightly on his forehead. "You're right, it wasn't flattering, and I'd just as soon not repeat it. But let me just say, it wouldn't matter if I weren't…." He lowered his voice. "You know," he whispered. "I'd never let anyone talk about someone else like that. Basically, they said if I sat with you all, people would start thinking things, and I told them they were right, but if I sat with them, people would think I was a moron."

Jacky howled—downright threw his head back and laughed to beat the band. "You didn't," he gasped, and then he began laughing again. People started looking over at them, and Jacky covered his mouth with his hand to try to contain his mirth. He failed. "Oh, God, that's good."

"Jacky, they're all looking at us," Simon whispered, mortified.

"Sorry," Jacky said, grinning at him. "You got guts, I gotta give you that, and you do realize you chose being at the light-in-the-loafers table over the macho cowboy table. That's going to get around."

"I can't help that," Simon said. "I'd like to think I'd make the same decision regardless of…."

"I know you would," Jacky told him. "You're a good person with a good heart. But I'm afraid you might have made some enemies."

"I was thinking the same thing," Simon said. Dante and Ryan returned and took their seats.

"Who made enemies?" Dante asked, and Jacky tilted his head in Simon's direction. Jacky told Dante what he'd said, and Dante nearly blew chili out his nose. Ryan passed him napkins, and Dante wiped his face. "It sounds to me like you've made a decision."

"Huh?" Simon asked, narrowing his eyes.

Dante looked at Ryan, who nodded slightly. "How about we finish eating? We can talk later, when there aren't so many people to overhear."

Simon returned to his food, wondering if he'd done something wrong. Jacky lightly bumped his shoulder and smiled at him. "It's fine," he whispered and then returned to his dinner.

By the time he was done eating, Simon could barely move, and God, his stomach was on fire from so much chili. He finished his second beer and wished for another, but followed Dante's advice and got water instead. The band continued playing, so Simon settled in his seat and just listened to the music. People began to dance, and Simon watched them, looking at Jacky, who swayed in his seat and moved his feet on the ground. Then he looked at Dante and Ryan, the two of them moving to the music. If he hadn't been looking for it, he wouldn't have seen it, the movements were so subtle. Then he turned to where the couples pushed each other around the dance floor, men and women having fun.

Simon stood up and stepped out from under the pavilion. After a few seconds, Jacky came out and stood next to him. "What happened?"

"Nothing," Simon said and walked away, the music softening the farther he got from the pavilion. "I was just watching all those people having a good time and realized I'll be on the outside forever. They get to dance, and I could tell you were itching to get out there and strut your stuff. Ryan and Dante too. But it can't happen. People won't accept it, not here and not back home either." It was like a light had come on in his head. He could see it all: the exclusion, being different, people pegging him and placing him in a particular box simply for being who he was. Simon clenched his fists and released them before doing it again.

"Hey, guys," Ryan said as he approached.

"Hey," Simon said without energy.

"Let's go on back to the trailer," Jacky said. "I think we could use another beer."

Back in their own space, Dante prowled like a caged tiger. "Sit down, you're making everyone nervous," Ryan told him, and Dante slid onto the bench seat next to him.

"What did you want to tell me?" Simon asked.

"You seem to have made a decision today, and for the record, I think it's a good one." Dante looked at Ryan and then back at him. "I was much the same as you until I met this one." Dante patted Ryan's hand. Simon still wasn't completely accustomed to the affection between them, but he was getting there. "You're lucky, because I was much older than you before I truly accepted who I was."

"I—" Simon said.

"Let me finish. I was a nationally ranked bull rider, and I was scared to death that people would find out I was gay. There had been rumors, but they'd died down. Then I met him and I couldn't deny who I was any longer. Ryan wouldn't let me. For a city boy, he was pretty cowboy stubborn. Eventually, I came out, but it was Ryan who paid the price for it."

"I think I heard about that. It was all over the Internet. My dad had some pretty strong opinions about it, but I can remember reading the stories when he wasn't around," Simon said. "Is that why you're so careful?"

"Partly," Dante answered.

"As Dante said, you seem to have made a decision, and it's a good one. Figuring out who you are happens over time; it's not some huge revelation."

"All I did was sit with my friends," Simon said.

"No, you didn't," Jacky said softly. "You made a choice to sit with us. You could have sat down with them and ignored their crap or even taken part to cover up. Lots of people do. But you didn't. You chose to be who you are. Sometimes in life, things happen to us and pull us in one direction or another. But the real life-changing events are the decisions we make."

"I guess," Simon said, leaning closer to Jacky. He really didn't see what he'd done as a big deal. But he did feel comfortable in his skin, something he hadn't felt for a very long time. "Can I ask you something? Did you all feel better once you came out?" The thought of telling his folks scared the crap out of him. He kept hearing his father telling him he was no longer his son.

"Coming out isn't about the people you tell," Jacky said. "It happens here in your heart. It happens when you allow yourself to accept who you are and the people you love. It's that simple. The rest is deciding to be honest with yourself and others." Jacky took his hand, and Simon vibrated with the energy that seemed to flow into him. "Each one of us has a different coming-out story. My mom already knew before I told her, and she loved me no matter what. Dante's grandfather didn't give two hoots and a holler."

"Gramps loved Ryan," Dante said softly in an unusual show of emotion. "He died about a year ago." Dante stood up and began to prowl again. Simon noticed that no one had talked about Ryan's coming out, and Simon didn't ask.

"You know," Jacky said. "I think that's enough of that particular subject." Jacky put his arms around him, and Simon leaned into the embrace. It felt good to be held. "It's getting late, and someone here has to ride tomorrow." Simon shivered at the way Jacky said the word "ride," like it was somehow naughty.

They all got ready for bed. Dante and Ryan pulled the curtain around the back bed, and Simon helped Jacky make up the table bed before pulling down the cabinet bunk. "You could join me," Jacky offered quietly as Simon stretched to pull out one of the pins. Simon paused, his heart racing. He pushed the pin back into place and stared at Jacky.

The bathroom door opened and Ryan came out, then silently slipped behind the curtain. Simon used that as a chance to escape. He hurried to the tiny bathroom and closed the door. He stared at himself in the mirror. He wondered if he somehow looked different, because he certainly felt different. Yes, he was nervous and still somewhat confused, but something deep inside felt settled, like a flutter that had been always been there had finally calmed. He ran some water and washed his face, then brushed his teeth. He still hadn't decided what he was going to do. Oh, he knew what he wanted: to step out of this tiny bathroom and right into Jacky's bed. But the war between what he should do and what he wanted to do still raged, although one side was most definitely winning.

Once he was finished, Simon looked at himself in the mirror and scoffed quietly. "You ride bulls and you're scared because you like another man." He shook his head at his reflection. "Good God," he whispered before opening the door. Jacky stood beside the bed, and Simon got out of the way so Jacky could use the bathroom. Simon looked at the cupboard above Jacky's bed, knowing he could undo the latches and make it into a bed. Once the door closed, Simon took off his shoes and the rest of his clothes and slipped under the light covers. He watched the door and waited for Jacky to come out.

The bathroom door opened, and Jacky stepped out. He closed it and walked to the bed. Simon saw a huge smile and then deep-blue eyes, and Jacky swallowed hard and then removed his clothes. Simon watched every move as more and more skin was bared to his view. Then Jacky climbed into bed and turned out the light above them. "What made you decide?" Jacky whispered, and Simon lightly tugged him closer.

"It was time to cowboy up," Simon said and then slowly rolled Jacky on the bed.

"Or maybe cowboy on top," Jacky quipped in a whisper, and Simon cut off further conversation with a kiss.

SIMON woke from a sound sleep and instantly knew something wasn't right. There were voices outside, and footsteps, when it should be quiet. Then he heard someone try the door and he bolted upright. "What…?" Jacky began, and then he sat upright as well. Jacky sprang to action and began pulling on his clothes. The noise woke Dante and Ryan, and they moved around in their end of the trailer while Simon hurriedly dressed.

In jeans, an inside-out T-shirt and bare feet, Dante charged toward the door. He unlocked it and pushed the door open. "What in hell do you think you're doing?" Dante bellowed and hurried outside. Ryan hurried out behind him, and Simon pulled on his shirt and followed Jacky outside.

Dante had a man on the ground with his knee on his back, and Ryan had another one by the arm. Simon turned toward the trailer and saw a red "F" sprayed on the side. The men had obviously been interrupted. "Get the officials," Dante ordered, and Simon rushed inside and stepped into his shoes. Then he took off toward the organizers' trailers near the stands. A single light shone outside the door, and Simon knocked. A few seconds later, a man answered. Apparently someone was up twenty-four hours, because he was dressed and seemed ready for trouble. Simon quickly explained what had happened, and the man grabbed a radio and requested help as he followed Simon across the rodeo grounds.

"What's going on?" the official asked, his hands on his hips as he glared at Dante, Ryan, and their two captives.

"These two decided our trailer was some sort of canvas," Dante answered firmly. "This one is so drunk he's already puked on himself and now he can barely stand up. The other one isn't quite as drunk."

The official nodded and stepped forward as others arrived. "We'll take care of these two. I think the sheriff can find them a nice place to dry out."

"I gotta ride t'morrow," slurred the guy Ryan had held.

"I don't think so. You're both disqualified from any events you were scheduled for," the official said firmly.

"Shit," the man groaned.

"Missing your ride will be the least of your worries by the time the sheriff gets done with you." The officials took charge of the men. "Do you want some help cleaning that off? It isn't dry yet, but it will be a bitch once it is. I think we have some solvent."

"I think we can clean it, but I'd appreciate the solvent," Dante said. "Thank you." He shook hands with the officials and climbed in the trailer. He returned with a camera while Jacky and Ryan got sponges out of one of the hatches. When the official returned, they thanked him, and once Dante had taken pictures, they began cleaning up the mess.

"Go back to bed," Jacky said softly when Simon reached for a brush. "We'll take care of this, and you need to ride in the morning. Get some sleep. We'll be as quiet as we can." Jacky dropped his brush in the bucket. "You being in top shape tomorrow is more important than cleaning off a little paint."

Simon nodded and went inside, then closed the door to preserve the air-conditioning. He got undressed, turned out the lights, and climbed back under the covers, then rolled on his side and closed his eyes. He tried to turn off his mind, but it kept churning. He knew what those cowboys had been about to write, and he'd recognized the falling-down drunk as one of the guys—and fellow bull rider—who'd been at Hank's table during the cook-off. He hadn't recognized the other man, but that didn't mean much. Simon yawned and tried to go to sleep. He heard the guys outside, though after a while those sounds faded as sleep took over.

The door opened and he barely moved. He heard the others moving briefly through the trailer, whispering a few words, and then after a few seconds, Jacky lay down next to him. The next thing Simon knew, it was morning, and the air was filled with the scent of coffee. He groaned and slowly sat up, stretching his back, which felt a tad stiff. Jacky was still asleep, and Simon thought about lying back down, but Ryan handed him a mug of coffee, which Simon took gratefully. "Everything okay?" Simon asked, looking toward the door.

"I didn't hear anything more, and Dante's already up and gone. He wanted to make sure our visitors got what was coming to them."

Simon sipped his coffee, the rich liquid instantly waking him up. "Why would people do that?" he asked, and then he wished he hadn't. He already knew the answer. "Sorry, stupid question."

"I doubt they'll get the chance to do it again. Dante will see to that. He was so angry he never went back to sleep." Simon heard footsteps and the door opened. Dante stepped in, nodding to him before turning to Ryan.

"The trailer's fine, no real damage, and I spoke to one of the other officials. He seemed to have this 'boys will be boys' attitude until I told him he could kiss any personal appearances good-bye." Dante prowled once again. "I also told him that I'd boycott next year's rodeo and would tell my friends to do the same. That changed the fat fucker's attitude mighty quick."

"Jacky's still asleep," Ryan whispered

Jacky groaned from next to Simon and lifted his head off the pillow. "Not anymore," he mumbled, and then he burrowed back under the covers. "What time is it?"

"Eight o'clock," Dante said in a normal voice. "Simon needs to check in by nine, and we'll need to be finding our seats if we want to get a good look, so get that butt of yours moving." Dante lightly slapped Jacky's rear end, and Simon growled. Dante smiled and stepped away.

"I'm getting up," Jacky said. "But if you don't want to be flashed, I suggest you clear out for few seconds."

"Come on," Ryan told Dante with a chuckle. "Let's give them a few minutes. Lord knows I don't need to see Jacky's skinny butt."

"It's not skinny," Simon said, "and you'd be lucky to get to see his rear end, because it's round and perfect. However, since you're both leaving, you'll be deprived of that view. Too bad." Simon crossed his arms over his bare chest.

"Feisty," Dante said. "Good. You're going to need that." Dante opened the door and stepped outside. Ryan followed, and then they closed the door. Simon got his bag and began pulling on his clothes. Jacky did the same, but paused as Simon stroked his skin.

"You do have a great butt," Simon said, exploring gently as he ran his hand over smooth, soft skin. "I have no idea where Ryan got that skinny-ass crap."

"It's because he has"—Jacky raised his voice—"old lady butt."

"I do not," drifted in from the other side of the door, and Simon smiled as he finished dressing and headed for the bathroom. He cleaned up, wishing he could take a shower, but it wasn't practical, not in that tiny tub, so he washed himself up and left the bathroom so Jacky could use it.

Once they'd cleaned up, he and Jacky stepped outside, and the four of them found a place for breakfast before he had to head over to the arena. Simon checked in, drawing his bull and riding order before nervously finding Dante.

"Which bull did you draw?" Dante asked.

"Widowmaker," Simon said, and Dante whistled. "What?"

"That fucker is aptly named. He loves to spin riders into a circle, drop them in the well, and stomp them. He's done it more than once. So be prepared. Remember how we practiced that and what to do," Dante said, and Simon nodded. "When we get home, I'm going to pull video from every single bull on the circuit. You're going to memorize every ride, and the behavior of every single bull. I should have done that earlier, but we were working on your riding. But half the battle is preparation, and we'll do that."

"I've got tons of videos," Jacky said. "I can bring a stack of competition DVDs."

"Good. Now, don't worry. You have hours before you're scheduled to ride, and you can either let the pressure get to you or keep it under control and let it drive you."

"Well, if it isn't the fruit contingent," one of the cowboys from the cook-off said as he approached the check-in window.

"Ignore him," Jacky said.

"Hey, faggots, I'm talking to you," he pressed.

Dante walked over and in one move had the guy on the ground.

"If you want to ride today, I suggest you shut your mouth," Dante growled. "All I have to do is call an official, and just like your little friends from last night, you'll end up sitting this one out down at the sheriff's office. Understand?"

"Yeah," the guy said, and Dante jerked him onto his feet.

"Now get lost. You can wait until we're gone." Dante pointed, and the guy paused before turning and walking away. "Hey, cowboy," Dante called after him. "Never forget you just got your ass handed to you by a gay man." The cowboy paused, then kept walking as Dante grinned. "Now that's how it's done."

"Come on, caveman," Ryan said as he took Dante's arm. "Let's go watch some rodeo."

THEY spent a few hours watching the calf ropers and barrel riders, followed by bronc busting. The entire time, Simon felt his nerves jumping higher and higher. "Remember what you did yesterday?" Jacky asked, and Simon nodded. "You need to focus on your ride and let the rest go."

"I know, but it's easier said than done. Yesterday I was just another cowboy trying to ride a bull. Today I have a shot, and I'm nervous as hell. What if I completely blow it?"

"You won't," Jacky told him. "You'll do your best. That's all anyone can do." Jacky lightly touched his leg and then turned his attention back to the arena.

Simon stood up and left the arena, moving to one of the back areas, where he tried to clear his mind. He needed to get his nerves under control. He breathed deeply and tried to push his fears away, but couldn't. "Simon," Dante called as he approached. "Think about what you're about to do and remember to let everything else go. Don't think about the score or winning. Just concentrate on the ride. It's what you came here for—not to win, but to ride. That's all that matters. We'll all be watching and cheering you on."

"I know. That's what's got me nervous. What if I really mess up?"

"If you get bucked, get on your feet and get the hell out of there. Don't stop, don't pause to see where the bull is, just run like hell. And when you're done, Jacky will be there to console you and listen to whatever you want to tell him. He won't think less of you, and neither will anyone else."

"But if I win…," Simon said hopefully, and the nerves started again.

"Then you win until the next rodeo, the next ride, and the next bull, when you could end up on your ass after three seconds. That's how this sport is—up one ride, down the next. It's that way for everyone. So take it one ride at a time, always do your best, and for God's sake, have fun. Because if it isn't fun, then hang it up." Dante turned and walked out of the area. Simon followed him, got his gear, and went to the preparation area to get ready.

"Look who it is," Hank sneered loudly as he came in. "You couldn't win on your own, so you had your fruity friends get the competition disqualified." He plunked his gear on a bench across the area from Simon.

"Quit being an ass," one of the other men said. "You and your groupies aren't going to get any sympathy around here. We all heard what they did." He turned back to his bag and began unpacking. "Dumbass," the cowboy added. "You're just jealous because the kid here rides better than you."

Hank looked about ready to blow his top, and if looks could kill, Simon figured both he and the cowboy would be dead. "I'm Frizz," he said to the cowboy, extending his hand.

"Diego Martinez." They shook hands, and Simon peeked at Hank, who was pointedly ignoring them, which was just fine with him. "That guy's a loose cannon."

"Then why antagonize him?" Simon asked.

"Because he's a dumb asshole," Diego said loudly, and when Hank humphed, Diego grinned. "He's been on the circuit as long as I have. A real loser. Never wins and rarely ends up in the money. His dad's some big shot in Houston and pays for him to ride, so unlike most of us, he just comes to these to get drunk and then try to pick up women. Riding is just a way to get some attention." Diego shook his head. "Mostly he's all talk, but…."

Simon unpacked and started getting into his gear. He was set to ride in about half an hour and he didn't want to be rushed.

"What did you do to piss him off?" Diego asked, and Simon told him about the encounter at the cook-off.

"I should have kept quiet," Simon added at the end.

Diego laughed. "You only told the truth." Simon shrugged and put on his protective vest. Then he slipped off his boots and put on his chaps before pulling the boots back on and taking a few steps, making sure everything felt right. Then he pulled his helmet out of his bag and set it on the bench. "You don't wear a hat?" Diego asked.

Simon shook his head. "I promised my mother I'd always wear a helmet. My uncle rode bulls, and he died in the arena. My mother near had a conniption when I told her what I wanted to do."

Diego plopped his hat on his head. "Ain't nothing wrong with keeping a promise to your mama." Diego smiled brightly at him, and after a second Simon realized what the smile meant. He flushed and smiled back, swallowing hard. An official came in and informed them they were starting. The first rider left. "You want to go watch?" Diego asked. Simon shook his head. "What bull did you draw?"

"Widowmaker," Simon answered blankly as he sat on the bench and tried not to throw up. Diego whistled, and Simon nodded. "It is what it is."

Diego gathered his bag and slung it over his shoulder. "I'm going to watch. Maybe we can get a drink or something later?" Diego smiled at him again and then left the room. Simon watched him go and saw Jacky stride across the area.

"What was all that about?" Jacky whispered quietly, but he was definitely angry.

"I think he was flirting with me," Simon whispered.

"Dante asked me to check on you, but I can see you're doing just fine," Jacky snapped, still whispering. "So I'll be heading back."

"Jacky," Simon said, totally confused.

"What?" Jacky asked.

"I wasn't flirting with him," Simon whispered as the light went on. Jacky was jealous.

"Oh," Jacky paused.

"Is this your boyfriend?" Hank sneered as he lifted his bag. "It's getting way too fruity in here," he pronounced and left the area. Simon saw most of the others nodding as they finished getting ready. No one said a word.

"I think I'm going to throw up," Simon admitted as he sat back down on the bench. "I've got people calling me names, and all I want to do is punch the jackass." Simon grabbed the edge of the bench, flexing his arms as he shook with anger.

"If you want to beat him, then do it out there," Jacky said softly, but with incredible intensity. "That's where you show how good you are and what you're made of. Calling people names is kindergarten crap. Daring to ride that bull is what you do. So let it go and throw what you've got into the ride. Dare to be the best and show him just how petty he is." Jacky grabbed his bag. "Come on. You're up soon." Jacky strode toward the exit.

"How'd you get in here?" Simon asked.

"Used Dante's name," Jacky said. "Worked like magic."

Simon left his bag with Jacky and carried bull rope and gloves down near the chute to wait for his ride. He watched some of the other riders, including Hank, get tossed around like they were nothing. Then he saw the handlers load Widowmaker into the chute. From ten feet away, Simon could smell him. The bull reeked of power, and damned if the dang thing didn't look at him and snort before tossing his head. When they were ready, Simon climbed on and settled on top of the animal equivalent of the space shuttle. Widowmaker's power radiated up through his chaps and jeans, right to Simon's balls. And it turned him on a little. Simon adjusted his hand and did a quick mental check before nodding.

Widowmaker practically spun out of the chute, going for the well right away and trying to spin Simon off so he could be trampled under his hooves. "You fucking pig," Simon cried and jabbed the animal with his spurs. Widowmaker jumped and leaped, twisting like he was possessed by the devil. Simon held on, nearly getting his arm yanked out of the socket, but he adjusted and gave the fucker another taste of the spurs. The bull ran forward and then came to a stop, trying to fling Simon over his head and onto his horns. Simon managed to shift his weight backward and stayed on by the grace of God. The buzzer sounded and Simon tried to bail, but as he did, Widowmaker jumped again, and he flew through the air, landing nearly flat on the ground. He rolled as best he could and then got to his feet out of sheer instinct and ran for the rail like the hounds of hell were after him. And right now, Simon figured Widowmaker was straight out of the seventh level of hell.

He reached the top of the wall, and the crowd cheered wildly. Someone shoved his hat into his hands, and Simon pulled off his helmet and waved to the crowd. When he looked, he saw Jacky standing near the base of the rail, beaming up at him. Simon smiled and waved to the crowd once again before climbing down. He collected his stuff and followed Jacky to where the others were sitting. "What in hell were you thinking?" Dante asked almost as soon as he sat down. "I can't figure if you were reckless or fucking brilliant the way you jabbed that beast."

"The score for Simon the Frizz is 94.33. That puts him on top, folks," the announcer cried, and the crowd cheered once again. Simon stood and waved one more time before sitting back down.

"I figured if I spurred him, his little pea brain would concentrate on that rather than spinning me into the well. Worked too," Simon said. His arm ached, but he wasn't about to tell anyone or even rub it, in case the officials were around. Dante had told him never to show pain to the crowd, so he sat and watched the next riders. Eventually, Jacky pressed a cup into his hand along with a couple pills. Simon dropped them in his mouth and downed a gulp of water before sitting back and waiting for the painkillers to take effect.

His arm felt better, but he was still as nervous as a cat as he waited out the remaining riders. Some were bucked, and others held on. Some scores were good, and each time, Simon listened for someone else to be declared in the lead. "It's going to be fine," Jacky said from next to him, and Simon nodded.

"That was one hell of a ride," the man behind him said and patted his shoulder. Simon kept himself from wincing as he turned around and thanked the man. "We've seen that bull more than once, and no one has ever spurred him the way you did. That was a thing of beauty."

"Thank you," Simon said, tipping his hat politely to the man and his wife. He turned to watch the last rider take off out of the chute. He watched as he was bucked around and then sailed through the air just shy of the buzzer. Simon's spine tingled and he shivered slightly. He waited and then stood up when he was announced as the winner. He waved his hat again and walked out into the ring, where he shook hands with the dignitaries and was presented with a check and a large silver buckle. He held it over his head, waved his hat, and smiled to the crowd. As he turned, his gaze zeroed in on Jacky and his brilliant smile. Even halfway across the arena, Simon could see him plain as day.

After thanking everyone, he stepped from the arena, and folks began filtering out. Simon made his way to where Dante, Ryan, and Jacky waited for him, and they headed back to the trailer.

The four of them packed quickly. Dante hooked the trailer up to his huge truck, and then they all piled in for the ride back to the ranch. Ryan spent much of the time on the phone, speaking with the ranch foreman and others to make sure everything was okay and running smoothly.

"You won your first buckle," Jacky said, bumping his shoulder in the cramped backseat.

"I almost can't believe it," Simon said as he pulled it out and ran his fingers over the design of a bull, the name of the rodeo, and date embossed on it. "I actually won."

"You had two very good rides, and I still can't believe you spurred Widowmaker. That's why you won, you know. It takes guts to ride bulls, but you shifted that and dared the bull to buck you." Dante chuckled. "We still have work to do on anticipation, but we'll get to that."

Simon nodded and settled back, closing his eyes.

"Hi, Mom," Jacky said into his phone, and Simon cracked his eyes open and then closed them again. "We're on our way back. We had a great time, and Frizz won his event." Jacky sounded as excited as he was. "He spurred him, can you believe it?" Jacky paused. "No, I don't think they televised it." Jacky paused again, and Simon yawned as he half listened. "Okay, I'll ask him." Jacky talked a little while longer and then hung up.

"How's your mom?" Simon asked.

"She's fine and wanted me to ask you to come to dinner next Saturday. She wants to meet you."

Simon snapped his eyes open and stared at him. "She knows?"

"Of course she knows. It's no big deal; Mom's really cool. Like I said, she wants to meet you. Will you come?" Jacky asked, and Simon saw Ryan peering over the seat expectantly.

*Cowboy up.* "Yes," he answered. "It just feels weird to think about meeting your mom."

Jacky laughed. "You won't after you meet her. Mom is so much fun. Remember, she's had me for a son. She's seen or heard just about everything." Jacky nudged him. "She's as big a rodeo fan as I am. I remember the first time she met Dante—she about wet herself." Simon wasn't sure what to make of that, but everyone seemed to find it amusing. "She's going to love you."

"If you say so," Simon agreed nervously and crossed his arms defensively over his chest.

# CHAPTER FIVE

THE rest of the ride back to the ranch was largely uneventful. Frizz called his parents and told them about winning the buckle. From what Jacky could hear, Frizz's dad seemed excited. His mother seemed less so, but Frizz was all smiles once he hung up. Jacky was tired, so he leaned against Frizz and curled an arm around his waist before closing his eyes.

The miles ticked away, and eventually they turned down familiar roads and pulled into the ranch drive. Dante let them out before parking the trailer. Then everyone helped unpack and haul the gear inside. "Are you going back to the city tonight?" Frizz asked Jacky, but he shook his head.

"I have tomorrow off, so I thought…," Jacky said, moving closer. "I thought we could maybe pick up where we were last night." Jacky was on fire. He'd spent most of the night, other than when he was cleaning off paint, pressed close to Frizz, and he'd been throbbingly hard all night long. He hadn't wanted Frizz to think he was being molested, so he'd done his best to keep things under control, but damn, it had been hard… literally. "It isn't a requirement," Jacky said, moving away when Frizz didn't respond.

"It isn't that," Frizz said as he took Jacky by the hand and pulled him around the side of the house. "Some things are meant to be private." Jacky nearly gasped when Frizz leaned forward and damned near kissed the life out of him. Jacky moaned softly and returned the kiss.

"I'll take that as a yes," Jacky said, swallowing hard after Frizz broke the kiss. He was quickly coming to realize that Frizz liked to be in control. "I think we should finish the unpacking and then help with dinner." Jacky tried to suppress a yawn, but failed.

"And I think we need to go to bed early. We've had plenty of excitement for the last few days, and I could use a little quiet time."

"I hope not too quiet," Jacky quipped, and Frizz laughed. They returned to the trailer and gathered up the last of their things. Dante directed the rest of the unloading, and by the time they were done, Jacky was exhausted, but he helped the others finish and then went out to the barn to help where he could before heading to the kitchen. He was by far the best cook, so he began making dinner. Ryan had gotten steaks. Frizz volunteered to man the grill, and Jacky put potatoes in the oven to bake and then cleaned vegetables and got them on to cook. Then he made a salad. For most people, that would be too much, but these guys had been active for most of the day and were coming off chores on top of it. They all needed to eat, so Jacky made plenty.

At serving time, Frizz brought in the steaks, and the four of them sat at the table with bottles of beer and toasted Frizz's success, though he looked almost embarrassed.

"Never forget to celebrate the wins," Dante told him. "You were the best there today, and you won because of it. There will be days when you aren't."

"I know. But I was brought up that pride is a sin and—"

"There's nothing sinful about wanting to win and celebrating when you do. Besides, I don't think that's the kind of pride they're referring to." Dante lifted his beer, and the others did as well, then they all clinked the glass bottles. They talked and laughed through dinner, chowing down like there was no tomorrow.

Jacky helped clear the table, and then Ryan and Dante shooed both him and Frizz out of the room. The two of them ended up in the living room, curled together on the sofa.

"This seems both nice and strange at the same time," Frizz said. Jacky wasn't sure how to take that. "I like this, being held and holding you. I just never let myself think it could happen."

"You never dreamed about it?" Jacky asked, and Frizz shook his head. "How could you not?" Jacky curled a little closer.

"I was taught that… this, between two men, was wrong, and when it did happen, it was merely sex to satisfy some depraved… base urge." Frizz was obviously having a lot of trouble explaining. "I'm coming to believe and understand that was wrong, but as a kid, I spent more time fighting what I thought was wrong in myself than I did imagining how life could be if I met someone kind and caring." Frizz sighed. "There are so many people I could blame for those notions, but they were just teaching me what they believe."

"It's a shame, though, to have any possible dreams of happiness and contentment ripped away from you."

To Jacky's surprise, Frizz laughed. "You don't know if something is missing when you never knew it could exist. I was happy because I was ignorant." Frizz pulled him closer and kissed Jacky lightly. "You opened my eyes and pointed out that ignorance isn't necessarily bliss."

Jacky said nothing. He knew Frizz had come a long way, but he still had a lot of fear and trepidation. Frizz had made some decisions, but Jacky wondered how those decisions would hold up when he was faced with the real test—dealing with his family and telling them the truth. As much as he wanted to believe Frizz would make the right decision and be true to himself, he knew the temptation would be massive for him to hide it from them. Hell, Jacky's mother had invited them to come for a visit so she could meet Frizz. He expected that even if they were together for decades, he might never meet Frizz's parents, let alone sit down for a meal with them. More than once he wondered if it was worth it, but then Frizz would smile at him and he didn't care.

It was on the tip of Jacky's tongue to ask what Frizz was going to do about his family, but he didn't. They were in a good place right now, happy, and Frizz kept smiling and then gazing at him with his incredible eyes. "Frizz," Jacky began as Frizz slipped his hand under his shirt, lightly rubbing Jacky's belly. "Maybe we should take this someplace else."

"Call me Simon. Frizz is the bull rider, and I don't want to be just that to you," Simon whispered and then kissed him hard enough to curl Jacky's toes. Then he slowly stood up and extended his hand, tugging Jacky to his feet. "'Night," Frizz… no, *Simon*… called to Dante and Ryan before leading Jacky down the hall to the room Jacky had been using.

Simon closed the door and wrapped Jacky into his arms. He tugged at Simon's clothes, pulling off his shirt before yanking his own over his head. "What do Dante and Ryan do when they disappear alone into the training shed?"

Jacky stilled. "Do you really want to know?"

Simon nodded. "Dante always seems so happy and calm when they come out."

Jacky sat on the edge of the bed. "How can I explain this…. Some people have needs that require more than just being together. What I know I was told in confidence and I won't betray that. But hypothetically, a person in control all the time might have a need to give up that control, to let someone else take care of him and let him feel vulnerable."

"I don't get it," Simon told him, and Jacky reached up and stroked his cheek.

"That doesn't surprise me," Jacky said and tugged Simon down to him, kissing him and pulling them onto the bed.

"It isn't whips and chains, is it?" Simon asked, and Jacky hugged him tight.

"The sweet things you say," Jacky told him, and Simon chuckled before climbing onto the bed. He got them situated with Jacky's head on the pillow and then kissed him hard. Jacky arched his back when Simon flicked one of his nipples and then winced when the pressure became too much. "Easy. Sometimes doing something lightly more than once is more erotic than hard and fast."

Simon paused and then lightened his touch, flicking Jacky's nipple lightly. As soon as he did, Jacky moaned and shook on the bed. Simon then licked his skin and wrapped his arms around Jacky's waist, holding him tight as he licked and sucked at each nipple. The intensity quickly built, and Jacky whimpered. "Am I doing it right?" Simon whispered.

"Beyond right; it's perfect," Jacky whispered and threw his head back when Simon licked trails over his chest and down his belly. His pants were way too tight, and he sighed and held his breath, holding in his belly so Simon could have better access to his belt. Simon opened it and popped the button on his jeans before tugging the fabric apart. "Please…," Jacky begged, and Simon stilled for a few seconds before sliding his hand into Jacky's boxers.

Jacky closed his eyes as Simon closed his fingers around his aching cock—the warmth, the firm grip, followed by light stroking, made his head throb with sheer delight. He'd been touched before, but Simon's touch was more intimate. Often sex was sex, and he'd had plenty of sex for the sake of having sex, but this wasn't that. Jacky hungered for Simon, and his skin tingled wherever Simon touched him.

"Love touching you," Simon whispered as he released Jacky's cock and went to work removing the rest of Jacky's clothes. Then Simon yanked off his own clothes before climbing back on the bed.

For a few seconds Simon simply stared at him, and Jacky shivered under the intense attention. "What's wrong?" he asked, feeling exposed.

"Nothing," Simon told him. "You're amazing," he added before slowly leaning in for a kiss. Jacky wrapped his arms around Simon's back and pulled him forward until they were hip to hip and chest to chest.

"I love touching you too," Jacky whispered and then flexed his hips so his cock slid along Simon's. He ran his fingers through Simon's wild hair and then tugged him into another kiss. "I want you, Simon. I want to feel you."

Simon stilled. "I've never…," he said, gulping slightly.

"I know. But I have, and it'll be amazing because it will be you." Jacky wrapped his legs around Simon's waist and then stretched to reach the bedside table. He pulled open the drawer and pulled out a small kit, which he handed it to Simon. "Use the slick on your fingers at first."

Simon opened the kit and found the bottle. Jacky watched Simon's unsteady hands as he squeezed some onto his fingers and then lightly probed Jacky's opening. He started with a single finger and then moved to two. Jacky moaned, and when Simon brushed over his spot, he gasped and moaned loud enough he was afraid Ryan and Dante might hear. Not that he cared. Over the past few years, he'd heard them on occasion, especially when Dante decided to bellow like one of the bulls he rode, but he didn't want Simon to feel self-conscious.

"Is this okay?" Simon asked.

"More than." Jacky groaned and clenched his muscles. "Roll the condom on yourself, use lots of lube, and go slow." Simon slipped his fingers from inside him, and Jacky instantly felt the loss of connection. Jacky waited while Simon fumbled a little, but then he slicked himself, and Jacky felt him press to his opening. Simon pressed forward, and Jacky's body opened to him. "Go as slow as you can." Jacky knew the temptation to go as fast as possible would hit any second. The delicious pressure and heat surrounding Simon would be too much, and as he expected, Simon sped up. Jacky was ready and relaxed as best he could while Simon sank into him, connecting their bodies. It was almost too much, and Jacky was tempted to ask him to stop, but as soon as Simon was inside, his cock throbbing in Jacky's body, he moaned softly, and they both stilled. "Move," Jacky commanded.

*Holy crap.* Jacky'd had no idea what he was in for. This might have been Simon's first time making love, but the man had rhythm. Simon rolled his hips and swiveled his lithe body, driving Jacky wild with passion. "Where did you learn to do that?" Jacky gasped breathlessly as Simon pegged his gland hard. Sweat beaded on his forehead, and he desperately clutched the bedding, feeling as though he would fly off at any second.

"I think of you as the bull," Simon told him.

"I think you're the bull," Jacky retorted, and Simon rolled his hips, making Jacky's eyes roll to the back of his head.

"No. You're the bull, a gorgeous bull, and I'm the rider. Together we're going on a journey," Simon said, and Jacky spent two seconds trying to figure out how Simon could be so coherent. Then all thought left him but Simon, his touch on his thigh, the way he filled him, and the throbbing that began at the base of his spine and zinged to his brain before making the return trip just as fast.

Jacky let go of the bedding and reached forward, stroking Simon's chest as he moved. He almost couldn't believe this was Simon's first time, but damn, the man was some sort of love god. "Don't you dare stop," Jacky told him breathily, and Simon leaned over him, stilling his hips. He kissed Jacky hard, then drove deep in a single movement while he feasted on Jacky's lips. It was almost too much. Jacky was coated in sweat, his cock bobbing and bouncing against his belly. He was afraid to touch it or he'd come in seconds, and he never wanted this to end.

Simon straightened up and resumed his fluid movements. Jacky could barely see straight or remember his own name. All he could focus on was Simon. Nothing else mattered or existed. When Simon paused and wrapped his hand around Jacky's cock, stroking as he moved, Jacky nearly lost it completely. Moisture ran down his forehead, and Jacky wiped it away, realizing his hair was wet from exertion. "Simon!" Jacky cried and gasped for breath, wetting his lips and then hanging on for more. Simon squeezed his cock and stroked faster and faster in time to the movement of his hips. Sensation on top of sensation threatened to short-circuit Jacky's brain. Spots appeared in his vision. Jacky closed his eyes and hung on, giving himself over to Simon, who continued the barrage on his senses.

"Jacky," Simon whispered.

"Yeah, now," Jacky said as the last of his control slipped away. Pleasure, pressure, and passion raced through him with mind-numbing speed. Jacky came, screaming at the top of his lungs. Simon throbbed inside him, and then Jacky remembered nothing else as he soared over everything and then flew outside of himself, floating softly, afraid to move in case the amazing lightness faded. Of course it did, and Jacky opened his eyes. Simon stared at him, and Jacky smiled up at him.

"Are you okay? Did I hurt you?" Simon asked. "You passed out, and I wasn't sure what to do."

"I'm fine, and I didn't pass out. You…." Jacky took a deep breath and sighed softly. "You were incredible."

"You scared me," Simon admitted. Their bodies separated, and Jacky groaned as the physical connection broke. Jacky swallowed hard and quietly explained how Simon should tie off the condom. Once that was done, Simon climbed off the bed and disappeared into the bathroom, then returned quickly with a washcloth and towel.

"I think we need a shower," Jacky whispered and forced himself off the mattress and into the bathroom. He'd hoped Simon would join him, but as Jacky started the water, the door, which he'd left ajar, didn't move. "Are you coming?"

He heard footsteps and then the door opened slowly. "I wasn't sure."

Jacky tugged Simon inside. "Showering after making love is part of the fun."

Simon closed the door and Jacky stepped under the spray, then beckoned Simon in after him. "Is something wrong?"

"No. I just feel like I'm supposed to know what to do, but have no idea."

Jacky let the water sluice over him. "You can't do anything wrong as long as you do what feels good." Jacky moved forward, up against Simon's body, and pressed them together. "Making love is about happiness and joy, not worrying about if you're doing things right. If you make your partner happy, you make yourself happy." Jacky picked up a sponge and motioned Simon to turn around. He lathered up and gently ran the soft sponge over Simon's back, then squeezed his buns before moving on. Then he had Simon turn around. He squeezed the soapy sponge and lather dripped out, running down Simon's chest and belly before dripping around and down his cock. Jacky placed the sponge in the soap dish and used his hands to stroke and wash Simon's chest and belly. Then he gently ran his fingers along and around Simon's cock and balls. "Just close your eyes and let me take care of you." Jacky continued working the lather. "Sometimes showering together and putting yourself in the hands of another can be almost as intimate as making love."

Simon moaned softly, and when Jacky was done, he did the same thing Jacky had, stroking and caressing Jacky's body. Once they were done, Simon gathered him into his arms and pressed his chest to Jacky's back, licking and kissing his shoulder as the water ran over both of them.

It began to turn cold, so Jacky turned off the water, but other than that, neither of them moved. Jacky closed his eyes and soaked in the caring warmth of Simon pressed to him. Slowly, Simon backed away and let his arms fall. He then pushed open the curtain, reached for towels, and handed one to Jacky.

They dried off and hung up the wet towels before returning to the bedroom and climbing into bed. The house was a little cool from the air-conditioning, which was fine with Jacky. He curled next to Simon, and after sharing multiple, tender kisses, closed his eyes and let himself dream that things could always be like this. He knew it was a dream that could pop like a soap bubble, but for now, it was enough. It would have to be. There were too many unknowns and things beyond his control.

ON FRIDAY afternoon, Jacky left the Western shop he and his brother owned in Houston as early as his slave-driver co-owner would allow and hurried to his condo. Simon was to meet him there, and then they were going to go over to Jacky's mother's. He'd been so nervous he could barely sit down the entire afternoon, and now that he was done for the week and Simon would be over in a little while, he could barely contain himself. Jacky pulled into his parking spot, grabbed his bag, and headed inside. After fumbling with the lock and dropping his keys, he made it inside. He rushed through the living room and down the hall to the small bedroom he used as an office and dropped his bag on his chair before hurrying on to his bedroom.

Jacky stripped off his clothes and jumped in the shower, because after they were done at his mother's, he fully intended to bring Simon back to the condo and get him to do another of his bull-riding demonstrations. He washed quickly and then got out, dried himself, and dressed. The buzzer sounded just as he was grabbing his shoes and socks, so he hurried out into the living room in his bare feet and buzzed the outside door open before pulling open his condo door.

Frizz… make that Simon—sometimes Jacky had to remind himself not to call him Frizz—walked in a few seconds later, and Jacky gawked, open-mouthed. He'd only seen Simon in jeans and either work clothes or cowboy clothes, but this was city-slicker

Simon in dress pants, a crisp shirt, and even dress shoes. "I wanted to look nice," Simon said, and Jacky pulled him inside, kicked the door closed, and kissed Simon hard.

"You do," Jacky said happily. "Boy, do you ever."

"I wanted to make a nice impression, and I didn't think jeans and a T-shirt would be right. I also didn't think I should wear a suit or something, so, I went down the middle. I hope it's okay."

"There's no need to be nervous. My mother is going to love you. She can be a little… outspoken… so don't be shocked by anything she says." Jacky sat in the nearest chair and pulled on his socks and shoes. "Sorry," Jacky said when he realized Simon was still standing. "Please have a seat."

"No, thanks. I'm just watching you," Simon said with a smile. Once Jacky was done and stood back up again, he made sure he looked okay, grabbed his keys, and motioned Simon out the door. He locked up and led the way outside to his car. Jacky unlocked it, and they got inside.

"Mom lives about half an hour away. It's only about ten miles, but it takes a while with traffic." Jacky started the engine and pulled out. "There's nothing to be nervous about. You ride bulls, remember?"

"I'm thinking that's easier than meeting your boyfriend's mother," Simon said with a forced smile. "I can stare down a bull or a horse, but this has me all tied in knots."

"There's no reason to be," Jacky said. "Well, okay. I know my mother is going to love you. She's a huge rodeo fan. When I was growing up, we used to go together, and after I came out, we used to compare notes on who we thought was sexier." Jacky laughed as he merged onto the freeway. It seemed to be his lucky day, because while it was busy, traffic was moving at a good speed. Jacky drove across town and arrived at his mother's house in near record time. He parked in the driveway and got out of the car. He waited for

Simon in the late-day heat, already beginning to sweat a little. Simon got out and walked around the car.

The front door opened, and Jacky's petite mother hurried out and down the walk before nearly tackling him in a hug. "You stay away for weeks at a time," she scolded, and Jacky returned her hug before stepping back.

"Mom, this is Simon," Jacky said, grinning. "Simon, this is my mother, Shirley."

"It's very nice to meet you," Simon said formally.

"It's a pleasure to finally meet one of Jacky's boyfriends," his mother said with a smile as she shook Simon's hand. "So how long have you and Jacky here been seeing one another?"

"We met over a month ago," Simon answered, and Jacky saw him blush.

"We met after a rodeo. I was there with Ryan and Dante. Simon was one of the bull riders, and he had a great ride. We actually first met at the bar after the rodeo."

"Well, come inside you two. It's hot as Hades out here, and I have dinner almost ready," she said before turning around and leading them inside and into the living room. "So you're a bull rider?" his mother asked once they were seated with drinks.

"Yes, ma'am. I really love it."

"This past weekend, he won his first buckle," Jacky interjected.

"I bet your family is very proud," his mother said.

"They're all happy this is what I want to do. My dad is okay with it, but my mom hates that I ride," Simon answered and then reached for his glass, his hand shaking slightly.

"Do they know about you and Jacky?" she asked, and Jacky groaned inwardly.

"Mom," he interjected. "Can we give him five minutes before you start the third degree?" He turned to Simon. "And she wonders why she doesn't get to meet my boyfriends."

"Excuse me, may I use your restroom?" Simon asked.

"Certainly. It's just down the hall on the left," his mother answered, and Simon got up and left the room.

"What are you doing?" Jacky asked as soon as he heard the bathroom door close. "Do you have any idea how hard it was to keep him from exploding from a case of nerves? He came to meet you because I asked, and you start the Spanish Inquisition," Jacky whispered forcefully.

"I don't want you hurt," she told him in the same whisper. "I remember the crap you went through with Juan. You cried on my shoulder for weeks."

"I know," Jacky admitted. "And I won't lie and say I haven't had those same concerns, but he's making an effort. Juan would never have come here in case someone saw him. The only reason you met him was because he couldn't avoid it when you visited and he happened to be in my room. Simon's a strong person who's starting to figure out and work through all the crap he's been fed all his life. I was hoping you'd show him that not all parents are like his." He heard the bathroom door open and changed the subject. "You should have seen it, Mom. It was an unbelievable ride. Even Dante was impressed, and he can be such a prickly bastard some times."

Simon sat back down and Jacky moved a little closer to him. "So, Simon, what do you like to do besides ride bulls?"

"Horses," Simon answered. "I've had one since I was about six."

"Do you have brothers and sisters?" Jacky's mother asked.

"Gosh, yes. I'm the oldest of eight," Simon chuckled. "My sister Ruth is twenty, then there's a big gap until my twelve-year-old twin brothers and four little ones. The youngest, Miriam, is three."

"Your mother is a brave woman," Shirley said. "This one was a big enough handful for me."

"We were lucky growing up. Mom didn't work outside the house, and Dad set up an office so he could work from home a few days a week. So we always had our parents around. I guess that made things easier for both of them." Simon grabbed his glass and took another drink.

"Simon's folks own Frizzell's Family Bookstores," Jacky said and saw his mother's eyes widen.

She nodded slowly. "Wasn't there some big brouhaha about them recently?"

"I'm afraid so. Dad terminated a long-time employee, and he's apparently saying it was because he was gay," Simon said softly.

"Was it?" Jacky's mother asked, and Simon shrugged. "So you keep wondering if he'll 'fire' you if you tell him." Simon nodded, and Jacky's mother tsked softly and shook her head. "Unfortunately, it happens. I can't understand a parent letting something as ridiculous as that affect their love for their kid. I know there's nothing Jacky could do that would make me stop loving him, except maybe vote Republican." She laughed, and Jacky saw Simon smile.

"I wish I knew how my folks would react, ma'am," Simon said.

"Please, call me Shirley, and I gave up trying to figure out the behavior of others a long time ago." She stood up. "I need to go check on dinner. I'll be just a few minutes." She left the room, and Simon turned toward Jacky, smiling nervously.

"I told you she'd like you," Jacky said. "So stop worrying."

"I hope you brought your appetites," Shirley called from the kitchen. "I made Jacky's favorite—enchiladas and rice."

Jacky's stomach rumbled in anticipation. "Mom's a great cook, unlike most of the people on the ranch, who would burn water. The last time he was here, Dante tried to con her into cooking for the ranch."

"I would have, too," Shirley said. "But you boys don't need me around spoiling your fun." She came back in the room, and they talked until the timer sounded. Then his mother got up again, and after a few minutes, she called them into the dining room.

Now that the ice was broken, Simon and Jacky's mother seemed to get along like two peas in a pod. They talked rodeo, bull riding, and about Simon's training until well after the dishes had been cleared. At the end of the evening, they said good night, and Jacky's mother hugged him good-bye and then shocked Simon by hugging him as well. She whispered something to Simon that made him smile, and then they headed for the car.

"What did she say to you that made you so happy?" Jacky asked once they were on the freeway.

"She said it didn't matter what anyone else thought, and that anyone would be lucky to have a son like me," Simon told him with a hitch in his voice. "I only wish it were true."

Jacky took one hand off the wheel and placed it on Simon's leg. "It is true."

Simon smiled and took his hand. "I know you think so. But my own parents will have a very different opinion, I'm sure." Simon released his hand. "My dad didn't fire that manager because he was gay, but he wouldn't have been looking for a reason if he weren't gay. I know how they both feel, and sometimes they can be so stubborn." Simon turned to look out the window. "He always talks about standing up for his principles, like they're the most important thing in the world."

Jacky laughed. "You realize that people who are always having to stand up for their principles are usually wrong and have to stand on their principles because otherwise there would be nothing left for them to stand on."

Simon turned back around in his seat. "My dad won't see it that way."

"How about we cross that bridge when we come to it?" Jacky asked, and Simon nodded. "There's no use worrying about it right now. He's in Oklahoma, and you're here."

"Yeah, there are more important things at the moment." Simon rested his hand on Jacky's leg for the rest of the trip to the condo.

It was late when they arrived. Jacky hadn't realized how long they'd stayed until he pulled into the quiet condominium complex. He tried not to yawn before getting out of the car and leading Simon toward the door. "How early do you need to be back in the morning?" Jacky asked as he inserted his key into the lock of the outside door.

"Dante isn't expecting me until noon. He said to tell you to come out as well and asked you to bring the rodeo DVDs. We watched all the ones he has in three days. By the time we were done, I thought my head was going to explode with so many bulls and riders."

"No problem. I packed them already." Jacky led them inside and closed the door. Then he took Simon by the hand and gave him a quick tour. "This is the living room, kitchen, dining area, office, guest room, bathroom, and, of course, master bedroom." He pressed Simon down onto the bed and brought their mouths together. Other than cries from lips on skin, whimpers from kisses that went on forever, and moans from touches that set their bodies on fire, that was enough talking for quite a while.

After making love and falling into a sated sleep, Jacky woke in the middle of the night to a thunderstorm. Simon shifted next to him. Jacky listened to Mother Nature's symphony and watched her version of fireworks out the window until Simon pulled him close and then rolled them on the bed, pressing him into the mattress. They made love to the rhythm of the storm, with Simon rolling his hips as thunder rumbled around him. And at the apex of the storm, when the building vibrated with the energy released, Simon rocked Jacky's world by driving forcefully deep. Nature seemed to be echoing their passion, and as Jacky reached his peak, thunder cracked and rolled, carrying their cries of passion toward the heavens.

The storm abated, and Jacky lay on the damp sheets, wrung out and covered in sweat. The thunder now rumbled in the distance. They got up and showered fast. Jacky quickly changed the sweat-soiled sheets, and then they climbed back into bed, as crisp and clean as the sheets. Jacky almost immediately fell asleep and heard nothing more till morning.

They ate a quiet breakfast together and then packed up before getting in their own cars and heading toward the ranch. Jacky drove a little slower and fell behind a bit. The drive gave him a chance to think, and whenever he did, a smile formed on his face. He pulled into the drive and parked next to Simon's truck. He expected to see him waiting, but the yard was deserted. He noticed a dark Cadillac SUV parked off to the side and wondered if Ryan was meeting with a client. When he got out, Jacky heard raised voices coming from the house and then the front door opened.

A strange man stepped out with Dante right behind him, carrying a gun. "Get the hell off my land or I'll call the sheriff."

"I'm not leaving without my son," the man said, and Jacky's blood ran cold. He had to be Simon's father.

"You mean your adult son who's old enough to decide what he wants?" Dante was smaller than the other man, but he was right in his face. "You get the hell off my land or I'll shoot you. I got plenty of witnesses that I was provoked. So try me. Go ahead."

Jacky watched as the man stormed off the porch and into his huge Cadillac. When he paused, Dante shot into the air. Jacky felt Simon's father rake his gaze over him, and he took a step back under the unabashed hatred. The man got in his car and took off down the driveway. Without waiting, Jacky ran toward the house, wondering what he would find inside.

# CHAPTER SIX

SIMON stood stock-still, unable to move or speak as part of his world—the part he'd feared losing—came crashing down around him. The hope he'd allowed himself to begin to feel, that his parents' love would overcome the news that he was gay, lay in tatters. His father had been more than clear about how he felt. Simon took a single step and his knees buckled. He grabbed the back of the nearest chair for support and stared out the front window. He heard Dante and his father yell at each other, and then Dante threatened him. The sharp crack of a gun discharging made him jump, and he nearly fell over. Simon wanted them to stop and to see if he could talk to his dad, but then he watched his dad storm away and his car take off down the driveway.

"Simon," Jacky called as he rushed in the room. He swallowed but couldn't seem to move. "Was that your father?"

Simon nodded once, and then Jacky had his arms around him, holding tight. "I'm sorry." Jacky held him, but Simon didn't move at first. Then he clutched Jacky to his chest, and they rocked softly.

Dante came in carrying his gun. He set it down and walked to where they were standing. "I'm sorry, Frizz. I couldn't let him treat you like that. Not in my house." Dante touched his shoulder, and Simon nodded before moving away from Jacky. "He probably went into town, and if you want to try to find him, I won't stop you. But he's not welcome here under any circumstances."

"But he's my dad," Simon whispered, barely able to talk.

"That doesn't give him the right to hit you or to try to run your life. I know I came on strong, but what I gave you was a chance for you to think and for him to cool off. Your father might hate me for the rest of his life, though I could care less. Let him focus on me for a while."

"I had really started to think it might not be so bad," Simon said. He wanted to break down in tears, but he'd be damned if he would do that in front of Dante and Jacky. Hell, he wouldn't give his father the satisfaction, even if he couldn't see it. "I should have known."

"Your father's angry and shocked. I'm sure he'll come around," Jacky said. Simon was becoming more and more convinced that he wouldn't. "Let's sit down, and you can tell me everything that happened." Jacky guided him toward the sofa, and Simon sat down. Ryan came in, carrying two armloads of groceries. He'd been at the store and had missed the entire incident.

"What's going on?"

"Simon's father was here, and I ran him off," Dante explained. Simon watched Ryan for a few seconds and then looked away.

"I'm fine," Simon said and stood up. He didn't need to bring down a whole trailer load of emotional manure on everyone. He'd moved to the bunkhouse from the main house a few weeks earlier. Maybe it would be best if he went back to the bunkhouse, or better yet, got some work done—anything to occupy his mind.

"No, you're not," Jacky said. "You don't need to put on the brave face or act all macho. This is hard, and we're here for you." Jacky moved closer to him.

"Let me put this all away and I'll be right back in. Then you can explain what happened, and we'll help you figure it out." Ryan hurried away, and Simon sat back down. It didn't seem as though he'd be going anywhere. What he really wanted to do was look for his father and see if they could talk.

"I need to find him," Simon said.

"I think you need to give him some time to think and cool off. He drove all the way down here and probably worked himself up really good on the trip," Jacky told him. Simon nodded. He could certainly see that. He sat quietly, the entire incident with his father running through his mind over and over. Ryan eventually came back into the room and settled on the sofa as well. "What happened?" Jacky asked.

Simon took a deep breath and swallowed hard. He wasn't really sure he could go into this right now. "Come on, you two," Dante said. "You're acting like fish about to go into a gossip feeding frenzy. Give him some room—he can tell you when he's ready."

Simon had never been more grateful to Dante than he was at that moment. "It seems my father got a call from someone who didn't identify himself, but he said he was someone I'd met at a rodeo, so I probably have an idea who it was. He apparently told my father enough that he drove down here to confront me. Dad arrived about an hour ago. I knew something wasn't right when I saw him." Simon sighed. "I can't go into this right now." His father hated him, he knew that, and there wasn't anything that was going to change it. He'd seen the way his father had looked at him, like he was the dirt under his shoes.

"It's okay," Ryan told Simon softly, and he got up and stood next to Dante. Ryan buried his face in Dante's neck, and Simon watched as Dante held him. Ryan had told Simon once how his family had rejected him.

"You need to be strong," Dante said, looking at Simon.

Ryan nodded and straightened up. "It's important for you to know that you haven't done anything wrong. No matter how your father feels or what he said or did, you aren't in the wrong here." Ryan's eyes blazed. "You are who you are, and if he can't accept that, then it's his problem. That has nothing to do with you, but it says a great deal about him."

"I wish I could believe you," Simon said.

"You have to," Jacky implored as he took Simon's hand. "He isn't right. It's the parents' job to love and accept their children for the people they are, not the people they want them to be." Jacky pulled him into a hug. "You aren't alone. No matter what, we're here for you."

"Thanks," Simon said as his mind began to shut down. He didn't want to think about this. All he wanted was to somehow make it all go away.

"Come on," Dante said as he moved toward the door.

"Where are we going?" Simon asked as he got up off the sofa to follow him.

"These two will have you assessing your feelings and probably lying on the sofa so you can tell them all about your childhood and why you hate your mother if you stay any longer." Dante pulled open the front door. "We're going to take this out on the bull." Simon followed Dante outside and across the yard to the shed. Inside, Dante turned everything on, and Simon climbed on the machine. Dante started it, and Simon began to move. He got in the rhythm of the machine and then signaled for Dante to speed it up. He needed everything he could get. Simon felt the machine speed up, and the crap from earlier faded to the background.

"Faster, Dante," Simon said as he felt "Frizz" take over, his worries slipping away as he shifted into bull-rider mode. Dante complied, and within seconds Simon flew through the air and rolled on the padding. The machine stopped, and Simon got back up and climbed on the bull. He motioned, and Dante turned the machine on.

He rode, got bucked, and rode some more until his legs ached and his back felt like Jell-O.

"That's enough," Dante said firmly when Simon began to climb back on the machine. "You're tired, and you'll hurt yourself if you keep going."

"I have more in me," he said, sitting on the mechanical bull.

"Frizz, that's enough," Dante told him softly. "It's time to quit and go back inside. I know what you're doing, but hurting yourself isn't going to make anything clearer in your mind or make the hurt seem any less." Dante leaned against the rail along one side of the building. "I'm the last one of this group of ours to be all touchy-feely, but you need to think clearly. I know this hurts and you were hoping for a different result, but what did you expect?" Dante stared at him.

"What did I expect? Fuck, I don't know. Maybe I was hoping the father I knew growing up wouldn't turn out to be a controlling asshole. That he'd at least listen to what I had to say. My father has never hit me before in my life, but he did today." The anger and hatred in his father's eyes had hurt much more than his fist.

"Yeah, he did, and I threw him out because of it. The two of you needed some distance, but you have to talk. It's the only way you'll find any resolution." Dante huffed softly. "I was lucky. Gramps loved me no matter what, and he accepted Ryan. Hell, there were times he and Ryan got along so well you'd have thought Gramps and Ryan had been friends all their lives." Dante opened a duffel bag in the corner and tossed Simon a towel. He caught it and wiped the sweat from his neck and face. "But it wasn't until after I met Ryan that I told Gramps. He didn't care, but the fear he would reject me had kept me hiding. There's no hiding for you any longer. It's out in the open, and now you can deal with it. Good or bad, happy or sad, you're better off." Dante came over to stand next to him and threw an arm around his shoulder, pulling Simon into a hug. "I know this sucks, but you'll get through it." Dante released him quickly. "Let's go inside before the others decide to send out a search party."

Simon nodded and followed Dante outside. Dante shut and locked the door, and they walked back to the house. The dry grass crunched under his feet, and Simon felt as brittle and dry inside as the brownish-green blades of grass. He hardly paid attention as he peeled off and headed toward his room in the bunkhouse. It was quiet; some of the guys were playing cards at the table, while others were probably finishing evening chores. He barely noticed them as he went to his room and gathered his things together for a shower. He ended up seated on the edge of his bed, staring at the walls in front of him. His mind whirled with worries, and his guts felt squeezed.

Simon jumped up and raced for the bathroom, reaching the toilet just in time to lose whatever food had been in his stomach. He heard one of the guys outside teasing about it being too early in the evening to be that drunk, but none of the others joined in.

Simon didn't move for a long time. He didn't have the energy. He only looked up from the floor when footsteps sounded behind him. Gathering what was left of his dignity around him, Simon stood up and turned around. Jacky stood in the doorway, worry and anxiety written all over his usually sweet face. "Come on," Jacky said softly. "Get your things and come on up to the house."

He almost refused, but when Jacky took his hand and pulled him forward, Simon didn't resist; he was too tired and churned up to care.

The other men watched him as they passed but said nothing, their usual conversation coming to a halt. From their expressions, he knew that they knew, and he wanted to crawl someplace to hide. But he couldn't do that, so he stood up straighter and pulled his hand away out of Jacky's. He wasn't a child, and he wouldn't be led off somewhere like he was helpless. "Just a minute," Simon told Jacky, and he walked over to the table, staring at the guys. "Do you have something to say?" he asked, looking at each of them.

"Yeah, man," Bob, one of the older men said. "We got your back if you need it." The others nodded. That wasn't what he expected, and Simon swallowed hard. "We're a family here, and we take care of our own."

"Thanks," Simon said, not daring to say anything more. All of the men nodded slowly, and then Simon turned away from the table to where Jacky was waiting for him.

Outside the bunkhouse, Simon strode across the yard with Jacky. At the main house, he stopped on the front porch. "I'm going to be okay."

"I know," Jacky told him and then swallowed. Simon expected to see concern and care in Jacky's eyes—he'd come to expect them from the kind man—but he wasn't prepared for naked fear. That almost made him step back. In a split second, Simon figured out the reason for the fear and opened his mouth to offer reassurance, but then closed it again. He couldn't honestly give Jacky the reassurance he needed because he didn't know what would happen. He couldn't even reassure himself. Jacky moved closer and then hugged him. Simon wrapped his arms around him and watched as the sun set over the grassland.

The door opened behind them, and Simon closed his eyes. "You two should come on inside," Ryan said lightly from behind them. Jacky released him, and Simon instantly missed the closeness. He followed Jacky inside and sat on the sofa, not really picking up on anything around him.

"What if I'm never able to see my brothers and sisters again?" he asked softly to no one in particular. "What if they grow up to hate me?" He continued staring at nothing and desperately wished he could somehow make everything right again.

"Should you call your dad?" Jacky asked.

Simon shook his head. "No. He's the one who charged down here and into Dante and Ryan's home." His anger began to rise. "He's also the one who decided to hit his son like he was a disobedient child rather than an adult able to make his own decisions. If he disagreed, he should have talked it over like always, rather than brandishing fists. So no, I don't think I should call him. He can fucking well call me if he has something to say!" He realized he was yelling and looked up as the others stared at him. His anger melted and he was suddenly extremely tired. "Damn it," he swore lightly. "I didn't mean to yell at you."

"You weren't. You were yelling at him, and that's healthy. You aren't a child any longer, and he needs to know how you feel. So if you want to yell, do it. Apparently he did enough yelling of his own," Jacky said.

That was true, but Simon had the feeling all the yelling in the world wouldn't make him feel any better, or stop his stomach from threatening to rebel every five minutes. At least he'd made a decision: he wouldn't call. Simon wasn't sure if it was childish or not, but his father would have to make the first move after that last encounter. He'd seen and heard about his father's business negotiations. His dad might have run a Christian-based company, but he was still shrewd and a hard negotiator. Simon had seen that more than once, so he knew a few things about his dad. Somehow he had to develop a position of strength, and this was all he had. What he had to be prepared for was the possibility that his father wouldn't call and that he'd never hear from his family again. "Yeah," he agreed after a few seconds and then lapsed back into silence.

"Jacky made some dinner while you and Dante were riding. Come on into the dining room and get something to eat," Ryan coaxed.

Simon wasn't sure if that was a good idea, but he got up and followed the others into the other room. He sat down and took a ham and cheese sandwich and a small bowl of tomato soup. He recognized the meal as Jacky's attempt at comfort food. He took a few bites of the sandwich and ate most of the tomato soup before putting down his spoon. "You need to eat," Jacky whispered to him, but Simon couldn't. He sat quietly and listened to the others discussing ranch business.

"One of the other ranches has some bulls they'd like to try out next week. They asked me if I'd give them a ride, but Ryan threatened my manhood if I did, so if you'd like, you can do it," Dante offered.

"That'd be great. Thanks," Simon answered with as much enthusiasm as he could muster. "Please excuse me," he said quietly and backed his chair away from the table. He left the room and went to sit in the living room, staring at the display on his phone. He'd blustered earlier about waiting until his father called, but he was so tempted to call him that he tossed the phone on the coffee table and turned on the television to give him something else to think about other than the infernal phone, which refused to ring.

The clink of dishes reached his ears as he settled in to watch whatever was on. Ultimately he ended up staring at the moving images, but not really seeing them. The others came in one by one and sat down, but he barely noticed. "Damn it," he said after a while and stood up. Thankfully, no one stopped him when he headed outside and stood on the porch. There was too much light, so he wandered around near the shed and stood in the open, staring up at the stars. He'd always been taught to look toward heaven when he prayed, so out of instinct, he looked up. The sky was filled with stars—hundreds, thousands, maybe millions of pinpoints of light. As a kid, he'd prayed for various things like a pony for Christmas or help on a test at school. Those prayers had been easy and simple, but now, he wasn't sure what to ask, how to ask, or even if he should be asking for what he wanted. So he stood and stared up at the stars and remained quiet as sweat coated his skin in the stiflingly hot air.

"If he's right, then I shouldn't be here…," Simon mumbled. "But I am, and I'm confused." He stood still, knowing it was unlikely he'd be given some revelation of clarity. Things didn't work that way, in his experience. Horses shuffled in nearby corrals, and in the distance cattle moved and called to each other on the still air. Simon closed his eyes and settled his mind, sending his wish and prayer silently into the cosmos. Then he opened his eyes and watched the sky. When he was a kid, his pony had gotten ill, and he'd run outside, looked up at the stars, and prayed for his pony with all his seven-year-old might. When he'd opened his eyes, a light had streaked across the sky, a falling star, and Simon knew he'd had his answer. He'd raced back into the barn and told his dad that Benjamin was going to be okay, that God had told him so. His father had ruffled his hair while the vet was with Benjamin. When he was done, he'd come out of Benjamin's stall shaking his head. Simon had rushed in and sat next to his pony's prone from and lightly petted him until his dad had forced him inside.

In the morning, he'd rushed to the barn, and seen Benjamin standing up in his stall, looking at him. His dad and the vet had talked outside, telling each other how surprised they were, while Simon had pulled open the stall door and hugged his pony. "God told me you were going to be okay. I knew it."

Simon opened his eyes and scanned the sky, but there was nothing—no streaking light across the skin, not even a special twinkle. Simon turned to go inside, and a breeze swirled around him, rustling the grass and caressing his skin. Then, just like that, it was gone, and he stood once again in the stifling heat, looking up at the sky.

"Are you okay?" Jacky asked from behind him, and Simon jumped a little. He'd been so deep in thought he hadn't heard the other man approach.

"Yes," Simon answered more sharply than he intended. "I was just thinking," he added in a softer tone.

"You were praying, weren't you?" Jacky asked, and Simon nodded. He'd never been shy about it before. "There's nothing wrong with it. I haven't prayed in years. I stopped after I was harassed by protesters outside a gay pride event. They wrapped themselves in the Bible and spewed hate and intolerance in every direction. After that, I…." Jacky shrugged.

"It's funny. I used to be involved with the church and everything they did," Simon said. "Youth group, Sunday school, all of it. Over the past few years, I haven't felt the same about it." He turned toward Jacky in the starlit darkness. "I guess I kept seeing myself standing on the outside, looking in. I'm still on the outside looking in, but now it's my family." Simon sighed. "I don't want to be on the outside any longer. I'm tired of it." He took a few steps back toward the house and then turned back around. "I'm sick of it. All my life I've been…." The exact word escaped him, and he yelled his frustration to the stars. "I didn't feel like I belonged because I always had this secret I had to protect. So I kept my distance and didn't let anyone, not even my family, see who I really was. Now that they know, I'm still on the outside, because they don't like who they think I am." He wanted to punch something. Instead, he clenched and unclenched his fists as anger rolled through him like oceanic storm waves. "It isn't fair."

"No, it's not," Jacky told him. "But you will always fit in here, and you aren't on the outside looking in—you're on the inside with the rest of us."

Simon smiled, even though he knew Jacky couldn't see it. "It's not the same," he said softly. "Not that everyone here isn't great, because they are. Everyone is wonderful, especially you. It's just that I want it all. I want to have my life here and I want my family to understand and accept me. Is that too much to ask?" Simon pleaded, addressing his question to the stars. "It certainly shouldn't be."

"No, it shouldn't, and your family should accept you for who you are. While we're at it, we could cure cancer, end hunger, and declare world peace," Jacky said. "The world isn't fair, and there's nothing we can do about it."

Simon's eyes widened. He'd never heard Jacky talk like that. Sure, he could dash off a sarcastic quip, but this was cutting, and he took a step away from him. "Jacky?"

"You have people here who care about you, and don't think for a second I don't know what you're leading up to. You'll cave and return home to live the way your family wants. That's what happened to me the last time, so why not this time too?" Jacky stepped closer to him. "Sure, the world isn't fair. So what? Do you really think the world should change because of you? It isn't fair to the rest of us either. For the second time in my life, I've fallen in love with a closet case who'll choose staying in the closet, or in your case, going back into the closet so you can be part of the family again."

"You love me?" Simon asked just before the air shot from his lungs.

"Of course I love you. Do you think I'm some tramp who sleeps with everyone who comes along? Who follows cowboys and bends over with my ass in the air like a cat in heat?" Jacky was yelling. "Of course I love you, you idiot." Jacky pounced and threw himself at him. Simon grabbed him, but Jacky had thrown him off balance, and they tumbled to the ground. Jacky held him tight, and then Simon realized Jacky was smacking him.

"Hey," Simon said and caught Jacky's hands. "I think I've been hit enough today."

"Then quit being a butthead," Jacky told him. "Because if you try to leave, I'll…." Jacky was shaking, and Simon held him closer, sighing softly.

"I know. I don't want to leave, but I don't know what I'm going to do," Simon confessed. "Everything is so messed up, and I'm so damned confused I don't know which way to turn."

"Fine, but going home and pretending to be straight isn't going to help you or anyone else. So just get that idea out of your head. You have to live your life for you and not your mom and dad." Jacky held him and rested his head on his chest. "They can't have you."

"Okay, so what do we do?" Simon said and then shifted and sat on the ground, holding Jacky to him. "We're still not any closer to figuring this out."

"Yes, we are. Because you've decided what's important to you. As long as you remember that, we can work together. But if you leave, you're on your own, whether you mean to be or not." Jacky stroked his cheek. "No one should be on their own. You might be a cowboy with all that loner stuff, but that's just dumb. You don't have to do this alone."

"Okay," Simon said as he got to his feet, and after helping Jacky up, they walked back to the house. "We'll do it together."

"You bet your sweet ass we will."

"I give up," Simon told Jacky with a chuckle. "You can stop the onslaught." They walked the rest of the way to the house and went inside. Dante and Ryan were watching television. Ryan leaned forward, picked up Simon's phone from the coffee table, and handed it to him. There were two missed calls, both from his dad. At least he'd called and initiated some form of contact. Simon stared at the screen for a full minute, wondering what he should do. He was so tempted to call him back. Jacky touched his arm lightly, and Simon stiffened his resolve. He slipped the phone into his pocket. Jacky took his hand and led him out of the room and down the hall. "I don't know if this is a good idea," Simon whispered when Jacky opened the door to the room he was using. Jacky stepped inside and tugged him along behind.

"I'm not saying we have to do anything, but you're not going to spend the night alone staring at the ceiling, wondering what's going to happen next," Jacky said more sternly than Simon expected. "I want you to remember you aren't alone." Jacky sat on the edge of the bed and pulled off his shoes and socks.

Simon was about to do the same thing when his phone rang. He pulled it out of his pocket and sighed before answering the call. "If you're going to yell, I'm hanging up," he told his father, and then he heard silence on the other end of the line.

"Is that how you talk to me now?" his father asked.

"It is since you decided I was a punching bag," Simon retorted, hearing more silence. "I take it you've calmed down some."

"Yes," his father said in a clipped tone. "But I think you can understand why I was upset."

Simon stiffened at his father's cold tone. "Maybe, but you should have been willing to talk, not hit. I'm not a child and I won't be treated like one."

"You're my son and you will act like it," his father told him forcefully. Jacky lightly touched his arm, and Simon remembered he had support.

"So when I disagree with someone, I should hit them?" Simon retorted. He figured he was probably beating the proverbial dead horse, but it was the only position he had that gave him any leverage. Simon knew it wasn't in his father's general nature to be physically aggressive.

"This is getting us nowhere." Simon heard his father sigh. "I'm staying at the Open Range Motel. It's on the edge of town. I'm in room 14. Why don't you come in the morning and we can talk."

Simon felt a surge of hope. He was about to agree when Jacky stepped in front of him and he rethought his options. "There's a diner just down the street. I'll meet you there at eight."

"We need to talk," his father said.

"And we can, but it will be someplace public," Simon said, and Jacky nodded slowly. Simon knew he was probably overreacting, but he wouldn't have guessed his father would have hit him either.

"I'm your father" was the reply, and Simon heard shock and disappointment in his father's voice. "Okay, I'll meet you there at eight." Simon hung up and put his phone on the nightstand.

"What's happening?"

"I'm meeting my dad at the diner in town tomorrow morning." Simon's stomach began to jump and churn, and what little he'd eaten threatened to make a reappearance.

"That's good. Talking is good. It's the only way."

"But…."

"He's willing to talk. He cares enough to sit down and talk with you. That's a first step. I'm starting to think your father isn't the biggest dickhead on the planet. He may be in the top ten, but he isn't the biggest." Jacky gave him a teasing grin. "Let's get ready for bed."

Simon nodded and got undressed. He settled under the covers and waited while Jacky used the bathroom. Then he watched as the door opened and Jacky walked naked across the room. His cock stirred slightly, but he was too worried to do anything about it. Jacky slid under the covers and curled right up to Simon. "Do you want me to go with you in the morning?"

"I think this is something I have to do on my own. I know I have your support, but I have to face my dad man-to-man." There was no other way around it. "I'm afraid if I show up with you, he won't really speak freely, and I think we need to be honest with each other."

"Okay." Jacky sounded disappointed.

"I know you're there for me, but I have to do this myself." Simon rolled onto his side and gathered Jacky in his arms. "Somehow I have to try to make my father understand that I'm the same person I was before he found out I'm gay. But I don't know how to do that."

Jacky was quiet for a few seconds. "Just be honest and say what's in your heart. He is your father and he loves you. If he didn't, he wouldn't have called three times." Jacky shifted and spooned to Simon. "You aren't going to make him see the light in a single conversation, and he's going to have a hard time. Those views you were raised with are the same ones he was raised with, and your dad has heard them for a longer amount of time." Jacky lightly stroked his shoulder, and Simon closed his eyes. "You also need to be prepared for him not to accept what you're saying." Simon shifted and sat up. "I'm not saying that will happen," Jacky hurriedly added. "But you need to be prepared for it, just in case it happens. Ryan wasn't, and it ripped him apart." The confidence that had just begun to build slipped away, and Simon stared at the wall in front of him.

"I don't know if I can be," Simon answered honestly.

"I know," Jacky said, and they lapsed into silence. Jacky kissed his shoulder, and Simon twisted so they could kiss good night, then shifted back onto his side. After a while, he heard Jacky's breathing even out, so he shifted away from him and curled on the mattress. Eventually Simon fell asleep, but it was fitful, and as soon as dawn lit the bedroom window, Simon carefully got out of bed, dressed, and headed outside.

He went to work on his chores, getting as much done as he could. When he knew the others were up, Simon went into the bunkhouse to clean up and change. The other guys came and went around him. Most nodded and smiled at him, and a few clapped him lightly on the shoulder as a silent show of support. Some of the men were gay, though most were straight, but it didn't matter—they were there for him.

Simon showered quickly and then dressed in comfortable clothes. He told Bob where he was going and when he'd be back before getting into his truck and heading toward town to face his father.

The drive went remarkably fast, and soon he was parked outside the diner, checking the clock on the dash. Ten minutes to eight. Simon could already see his father sitting at one of the tables. Simon got out and walked to the front door. He pushed it open and stepped inside. His father saw him almost immediately and stood up. Simon walked over to the table and waited to see what his father would do, and they ended up staring uncomfortably at each other, so Simon slipped into the booth. His father sat down as well, and the retirement-age server approached the table. She poured Simon a cup of coffee and then left to give them time with the menu. Simon cradled the warm cup in his hands but didn't drink from it.

"This is so hard," his father said, breaking the ice. "We've never had trouble talking before."

Simon lifted his cup and sipped. "I know." He set down the cup. "I don't know where to begin."

"Why don't you start with when you made this decision," his father began.

"I didn't." Simon lowered his voice, thankful no one else was in the tables around them at the moment. "Being gay isn't something you decide." He huffed. "Do you think I would choose to disappoint you like this, or to be the subject of harassment? You're smarter than that, Dad."

"Don't be smart," his father chided.

"Then don't say stupid things," Simon challenged, immediately wishing he hadn't. That wasn't going to help. "I've known for a long time, and I've been trying to come to terms with it, including how to tell you and Mom, but I could never figure out how to tell you something you'd hate me for."

"Was it the people here? Are they to blame?" his father asked. "If I'd have known, I never would have let you come to work here."

Simon leaned across the table. "Dad, I ride bulls. I sit on top of fifteen-hundred pounds of muscle and dare it to buck me off. I fucking spurred Widowmaker, the highest-ranked bull in the competition, not once, but three times. I'm my own man, and I'm not going to let you make my decisions for me any longer."

"Are you prepared to walk away from your family?" his father threatened.

Simon knew this was the moment of truth, the one he'd dreaded. "I won't walk away from my family, but it sounds like my family is walking away from me." Simon barely stopped to breathe. "Do you love me, Dad?"

"You know I do," his father answered.

"Then you'll have to love me for who I am instead of who you want me to be. I'm a gay man, Dad. I didn't choose it, but it's what I am." Simon quieted as the server approached the table. Simon ordered some fruit, and his father ordered the breakfast special. "It's been hard accepting who I am, and I'm not sure I can ever be truly comfortable with it, but that doesn't change facts. I've had the support of some very good people."

"I met some of those people," his father countered. Simon scoffed. He'd spent most of the night wondering how this conversation would go. He'd never imagined this. "They weren't exactly—"

"They were protecting me from someone I shouldn't need protection from," Simon interrupted.

"But this is wrong—acting like this is wrong. You know that. Your mother and I raised you properly, with proper values. Not like this…." He waved his hand at nothing.

"What's wrong with me being who I am?" Simon shook his head. "I love you, Dad, but I believe you're wrong." Never in his life had Simon said something like that to his father. His father's eyes widened, and he stared at Simon in apparent disbelief. "I've come to realize that some of what I was taught was wrong."

The server approached and placed a small bowl of fruit in front of Simon and a plate of bacon, eggs, and pancakes at his father's place.

"It's wrong, the Bible says so and you know it," his father said.

Simon reached across the table and snatched the three pieces of bacon from his father's plate. "What are you doing?" his father asked, trying to take back his food.

"The Bible says eating pork is unclean. So you can't have this. The Bible says so." Simon met his father's astonished stare. "Your hypocrisy is showing." Simon put the bacon back on his dad's plate.

"Simon," his father growled, and Simon remembered riding that bull and coming out on top.

"It's an example that maybe not everything is as cut-and-dried as you might want it to be." Simon looked up as the door to the diner opened and saw the guys from the ranch file in, including Jacky, Dante, and Ryan. They filled all the empty tables on the other side of the diner. His father turned around, probably to see where he was looking.

"Are they here to make sure you don't defect?" his father asked, and Simon laughed. He couldn't help it.

"Listen to yourself," Simon told him. "You sound like a crazy person." His father whipped around.

"I will not be insulted," his father said and pushed his plate away.

"Did it ever occur to you that they're here as support? Most of those people aren't gay." That seemed to shock his father. "They're the people I work with, and they took time away from the ranch to make sure I'm okay. They care about me." Simon smiled when he saw Jacky grinning at him. "And for the record, no one recruited me, but they did try to help me work through my feelings," Simon continued. "Feelings I've had since I was fourteen and didn't understand." Simon took a few bites of fruit, but was no longer hungry. "I never fit in and always felt different from the other kids, and now I know why. You might not be happy about it, but at least I understand why I never fit in with the other kids and why I always felt like I was on the outside. I was different. But I'm still your son and the same person I've always been. I'm just being honest now, with you and with myself." Simon stood up. "I don't know if you can accept me or not. I hope you can, because I want to be a part of my family." Simon took a step.

"You're walking away?" his father asked from behind him.

"Either you accept me or you don't. There isn't much more I can say. I won't come home and hide any longer; I can't do that. I also won't have anything to do with one of those quack therapies that the minister or anyone else comes up with. That isn't going to happen. I am who I am, and I have people who are willing to accept me at face value without conditions. You have to decide what you want. I know I can't say anything to convince you, as much as I want to try."

"So you're just going to leave," his father said, standing up.

Simon stepped back to him. "I know what you want, Dad. You want me to say I was wrong and to come home and do what you want me to do. You want me to be exactly the person you see me as. But I can't. I'm not that person and I've never been that person. I've lied to you and hidden who I was from you for years because I knew you didn't want to hear it. Well, I can't do that any longer. I am who I am."

His father placed some money down on the table, turned, and walked toward the door of the diner without turning around. Simon stared after him, almost unable to believe what he was seeing, and yet it was what he'd expected all along. He'd thought his father finding out about him and rejecting him would be the worst thing that could happen to him. He'd been afraid of this exact situation, and now that it had happened, he felt numb, and in a strange way, relieved. At least he knew what his father thought of him.

The door to the diner closed behind his father, and Simon walked to where his friends waited, having watched the entire exchange, as had half the occupants of the diner. He approached them slowly, praying his knees didn't give out.

"It'll be okay," Jacky said, tugging him into the booth next to him. "I bet your dad will come around."

"What makes you say that?" Simon asked, looking out through the window as his father got in his car and pulled out of the parking lot. "Dad's so sure he's right most of the time, especially about things like this. He sees some things as black and white."

"Maybe, but he listened to you. He didn't get up right away. That's a start," Jacky told him, and Simon nodded. "Give him a chance to think things over."

Ryan lightly touched his hand. "It's one thing to be angry and quite another to turn your back on the child you raised. My folks never listened to anything I had to say. After I told them, they refused to see me any longer. But for the record, I think Jacky's right. I saw the look on your dad's face. There's a war going on inside him. He loves you, but he can't reconcile the whole gay thing. Try giving him time and then give him a call."

Simon nodded and stared blankly at the table. Things had to work out. The thought of not being able to see his mother, or his brothers and sisters, as well as his father again sent him down a slope of despair. His family had been the center of his life, and now it seemed very likely it was cut off from him. "It's a huge price to pay to be true to yourself," Simon said softly, and a whispered chorus of amens sounded around him.

It took about five minutes for the worry to really kick in, and then the second-guessing began. Simon stared out the diner window, wondering what he'd done. His father was gone, and he didn't know if he'd ever hear from him again. Would he be able to see Miriam again and hear her laugh? Would he roughhouse with Jeremiah and Malachi again, or would they come to hate him for who he was? He went through the rest of the family, wondering, and with each one, his despair grew. Maybe it would have been easier to go home and hide. Suddenly, he desperately needed fresh air. He stood up, hurried outside, and gulped the morning air. He stepped over to his truck and opened the door, doubling over as he vainly tried to get enough air.

"Slow and easy," Ryan said from behind him and gently placed his hand on Simon's back. "Don't gulp, but breathe slow and easy. In… and out, in… and out." The tightness in his chest lessened and slowly eased away. He stood up and continued breathing carefully. "It's okay. You were having a panic attack."

"I'm sorry for being such a girl," Simon said, and to his surprise Ryan laughed softly.

"Damned cowboys," Ryan said, still chuckling. "You all think because you can ride a horse or spend eight seconds on a bull that you can control your emotions, or worse yet, shouldn't have them at all. It doesn't work that way."

Simon nodded. "I think I messed up."

"Because you told your dad how you felt?" Ryan asked, and Simon nodded as the tightness began to return. "He needed to know." Ryan sighed. "Sometimes there's a price to pay for being true to yourself. It's not fair, but that's the way it is. I paid it, same as you. I haven't spoken to my family in a long time, and I probably never will again. To tell you the truth, I know my parents are alive, but I don't know if they're in good health. I don't know if they think of me sometimes or if they regret their decision and are too proud to admit it."

"How'd you get through it?"

"Jacky," Ryan said. "He's one of the most supportive and caring people I've ever met. And I can tell you, you're lucky to have him in your life."

"I know," Simon whispered as he thought about how close he'd come to leaving. He looked through the diner window and saw Jacky looking back at him. Simon smiled and Jacky returned it.

"It's a pretty magic thing when you find someone who loves you, and while it doesn't make up for all of the loss, it sure goes a long way," Ryan told him.

"Do you have any regrets?" Simon asked.

"Every day, but not about being honest with myself, and not about loving Dante. Those decisions were the right ones. And yes, I paid a price for the first one, but the best night of my life was the one when Jacky dragged me to the bar after the rodeo and I caught sight of a certain rodeo cowboy." Ryan lightly squeezed his shoulder. "Let's go back inside."

Simon followed Ryan back into the diner. His phone buzzed as he was about to sit back down. He pulled it out and saw a text message. It was from his father:

*Heading home. Good-bye.*

# CHAPTER SEVEN

SIMON was silent after he returned from talking with Ryan. He'd sat next to Jacky, but had said nothing, and Jacky was beginning to worry. The other guys had noticed as well and kept shifting their gazes to where Simon sat staring at his phone. Eventually he put it away, but then he just stared down at the table.

"We should get back and go to work," Dante said as he scooped the check off the table and ambled over to the cashier to pay for breakfast.

Jacky was surprised when Simon handed him his keys. "Drive by the motel down the street," he said, and Jacky nodded before getting in the truck. He adjusted the seat slightly and then started the powerful engine and pulled out of the lot. Jacky drove slowly past the hotel, but the car he'd seen at the ranch wasn't there. He glanced at Simon and saw his shoulders slump a little more. This was not good. Simon had energy and a spark—it was part of what Jacky loved about him—but now that spark seemed to be missing. As Jacky drove out to the ranch, Simon almost slumped in his seat. A few times, Jacky expected him to fall over as he took the turns.

He reached the ranch and pulled into the driveway, then parked near the bunkhouse in Simon's usual spot. He opened the door, and

Simon did the same. The others arrived, and the men piled out of the vehicles and headed off to work. Simon simply looked around and then walked blankly into the barn. Jacky moved to follow him.

"Let him go," Ryan said from behind him. "He needs to work through this on his own."

"But…."

"Remember what you did for me when this happened?" Ryan asked, and Jacky nodded. "You have to give him the same space. I know it's hard, but he needs to think things through. He'll probably work himself to exhaustion, which isn't a bad thing either. The anger and frustration will kick in after a while as well, and he'll be a bundle of nerves. So give him time. He'll find you when he's ready." Ryan chuckled. "Do you remember pulling me into the shower in my clothes after I'd sat around for almost three days?"

"Yeah," Jacky said. "But if he does that, you get to turn the hose on his smelly ass. I did it for you, and now you need to pass on the love… and take a turn with the stink." Jacky watched as Simon shuffled into the barn.

"You want me to get Simon in the shower? That probably wouldn't go over well with Dante," Ryan said, lightly bumping Jacky's shoulder. "Just give him time." Ryan walked away, and Jacky debated going after Simon, but instead went to sit on the porch, where he could watch the barn without appearing to watch the barn. He sat down and stared over the grassland, watching as dark spots slowly moved over the land.

Eventually, he went inside and got a glass of sweet tea before returning to the porch. He'd just sat back down when an older blue Malibu pulled into the drive. Jacky watched as the car pulled up to the house and stopped. Then a young man got out, plunked a cowboy hat on his head, and ambled up to the porch, almost like a character out of a movie.

"I'm looking for Simon. You might know him as Frizz," the young man said.

"What do you want with him?" Jacky asked without getting up.

"I'm a friend of his from back home. I heard about what happened and hightailed it down here. I figured he'd need a friend." He pulled off his hat. "Name's Gardner. Is he here?"

"That depends on if you're here to cause him more grief," Jacky said, standing up to look the other man in the eye.

"Heck, no. He's my oldest friend. We went to rodeos together until he moved down here. I heard around town what had happened and knew he'd need support, especially if his dad had come down here to rip into him."

"He's in the barn," Jacky said. "Why don't you have a seat? He's had a heck of a morning, and I'm hoping he'll be done working out his grief soon." Jacky's instinct was to go looking for Simon, but he'd decided to follow Ryan's advice.

Gardner sat down slowly. "Is he okay?"

"I don't know," Jacky answered honestly. "If you're his friend, then you've seen that fire he has when he's excited. Like he knows what he wants and he can do anything?"

Gardner smiled. "Yeah, I know what you mean."

"This morning, after his dad left, it was like someone blew out the flame. He was quiet, slumped down, and didn't seem to care. When we got home, he went into the barn and hasn't come out since except to dump muck on the pile." He suddenly remembered his manners. "I'm Jacky, by the way."

"I figured that. He's called a few times, and somehow the conversation always seemed to come around to you," Gardner said.

"Did you know… about him?" Jacky asked.

"Yeah. He told me once in a moment of weakness. I didn't care, but we both knew his folks would. When I heard he was coming here, I was both scared for him and excited because he might be able to find some peace. I always thought he rode bulls as an outlet for his confusion. He got to take on a part of the world." Gardner looked over toward the barn, and Jacky followed his gaze. Simon had come out of the barn. Gardner slowly descended the steps and met Simon in the yard. Jacky watched as the two of them hugged. He saw them speaking softly, but couldn't hear what they said. Whatever it was, Simon seemed a little more himself when they joined him on the porch.

"This is Gardner," Simon said as they sat down.

"Jacky and I met while you were working out your frustrations," Gardner explained.

"What are you doing here?" Simon asked.

"I heard what happened from Ruth and drove down," Gardner explained. Jacky watched the two of them together and tried not to get carried away. When Gardner moved close to Simon, Jacky wanted to smack him. "I also wanted to tell you that I met a girl a few weeks ago. She's a barrel racer, and let me tell you, she's something else. I brought her to meet Dad, and the two of them hit it off real good."

"You brought a girl to meet your dad? This must be serious," Simon said, and Jacky relaxed. "So why aren't you with her? I appreciate you coming down and all, but I'll be okay."

Jacky stood up and left the two of them to talk. He didn't need to hear their conversation. Inside, he flopped on the sofa and stared up at the ceiling.

"Who's that with Simon?" Dante asked as he walked through the room toward the door.

"Friend of his. I figured I'd let them talk. I wasn't doing him any good, but Gardner seems to be helping."

"Don't sulk," Dante told him. "Simon needs you. He just needs someone to talk to that he isn't involved with. If they're old friends, then that could help." Jacky knew Dante was right, but he still wished Simon were talking to him. He heard their voices drift in when Dante opened the door and then cut off when he closed it again. Jacky watched television for a while and then wandered back outside. Simon and Gardner had moved off the porch, and Jacky found them wandering through one of the pastures. He approached, and Simon came over to him and placed his arm around Jacky's waist.

"I wish I could tell you he'd come around," Gardner said. "But I don't know anything more than you do. Just take it one day at a time and do your best to move on. Your father can be generous to a fault, but he can also be a pain in the ass. He didn't happen to mention that he's being sued by that guy he fired, did he? It's big news back home, and your dad isn't getting much public support. Times have changed, and people don't take kindly to that kind of thing."

Simon leaned against Jacky. "All I can do is wait and see what happens. The ball is in his court, and I can't change his mind, no matter how much I might want to. He's going to think what he wants. It doesn't make it any easier, but it's the truth."

"What are you going to do?" Gardner asked.

"I don't think there's anything I can do," Simon said, and Jacky could almost see him deflate. Some of Simon's energy had returned, but it seemed to drain away again. Simon dropped his arms and moved away. "I have some things I have to get done."

"I'll come with you," Gardner said, and Jacky headed back toward the house. If Simon wanted to spend time with his friend rather than him, there was nothing Jacky could do about it. He flopped on the sofa and ended up spending much of the rest of the morning watching television.

"He needs time," Ryan reminded him more than once as he passed through the house.

"I know," Jacky said, but it felt as if Simon was pulling away. Maybe he was being ridiculous. After all, Simon was just spending time with an old friend, and the guy was straight, so there was nothing for him to be jealous of. But it felt like Simon didn't want him around. At least he and Ryan got to spend some time together. They'd both been busy, so it was good to catch up. At lunchtime, Jacky helped with the cooking. He hoped Simon would join them, but when he'd returned from the ride, Jacky had noticed Simon's truck was gone, so he figured Simon and Gardner had gone into town. More than once he reminded himself that he and Simon weren't joined at the hip, but he knew Simon was hurting, and it hurt that Simon was staying away. Jacky wanted to be able to help.

At some point in the afternoon, Jacky heard Simon's voice in the yard and peered through the window to see Simon and Gardner heading back toward one of the pastures. "You know he's just spending time with his friend," Ryan said.

"I know I'm being dumb, but I want to be there for him," Jacky said.

"Then be there. Simon said his friend has to go home tomorrow. He can't stay very long, and then Simon's going to be alone again. Having Gardner here is probably lessening the hurt of his dad's rejection."

"You're probably right," Jacky said and headed outside. As he approached where Gardner and Simon were watching one of the horses, he said, "Do you feel like a ride on the bull?"

Simon shook his head. "I don't think I can concentrate right now." He didn't even look at him. Jacky moved next to Simon and leaned against the fence, watching the horses. This time, Simon didn't touch him or even seem to notice he was there. The only consolation was that he seemed to be ignoring Gardner as well. "I was always so scared of this happening, and now that it has, it doesn't seem real." Simon let his head hang low, and Jacky touched his hand to let him know he was there. But Simon ignored him and continued staring.

"You could just tell your dad it was a mistake and that you're really normal," Gardner said, and Jacky ground his teeth. He was about to argue the point when Simon spoke up.

"No, I can't, and you know it. Do you remember when you first noticed girls?" Simon asked Gardner, and he nodded. "Well, I noticed boys. This isn't some decision I made—I thought you knew that. Besides, I'm not going to lie. Yes, it hurts that my father wasn't accepting, but it would hurt worse if I went home and pretended everything was perfect and I'd made some horrible mistake. And while I'm at it, I could dress up as a unicorn and have rainbows shoot out my ass!" Jacky stared openmouthed at Simon. That last line had so many connotations Jacky couldn't help laughing.

"Dude," Gardner said, and then he broke down laughing too, doubling over. "You don't have to dress up as a unicorn to have rainbows shooting out your ass." Gardner laughed harder, and Jacky saw Simon look at him blankly. Jacky explained about the rainbow flag and what it meant between gasps for air, and quickly calmed himself when Simon simply stared at him. "Come on, dude, it was funny."

"I'm sorry if I don't feel like laughing," Simon said morosely, and Jacky sighed.

"Come on, Simon. I know you're hurting, but it will get better," Jacky said. "I'm not sure how or when, but it will. For now, try not to concentrate on it and go on into the shed. Dante is probably over there, and you can take your mind off all this. It will give you something else to think about."

Simon nodded and pushed back from the railing. He and Gardner walked to the shed, which appeared to be open, and Jacky went into the barn. He needed to find something to do. This was not the weekend he had envisioned at all. He'd been hoping for a fun weekend, maybe a little riding, and making love in the shade of one of the trees near the creek. Jacky sighed. He knew no relationship was roses and sunshine all the time, but this was almost too much. He thought about packing up and going back to the city, and he even began walking back toward the house, but stopped in the middle of the yard. The night before, he'd exacted a promise from Simon that he wouldn't run home and leave him, and Jacky would be damned if he'd do the same thing to Simon. Making a decision, he strode over toward the shed and peered inside. Gardner was riding the bull, and Simon was watching. Jacky moved next to him and took his hand, entwining their fingers.

Gardner went flying and landed on the padding before rolling deftly to a stop. "You know, it's going to be okay," Jacky said, looking at Simon. "It doesn't feel like it right now, but it will be. You being gay isn't the end of the world. Right now it feels that way to you, and to your family, but it won't always be that way."

"How do you know?" Simon asked.

Jacky shrugged. "I can feel it here." He placed his hand on Simon's chest. "You have a good heart, and you got it from them. Everything feels raw and chafed right now. Your emotions are on edge, and so are theirs. Give them some time and give yourself some time."

"I think I should go home and try to work this out," Simon told him, and Jacky nodded slowly.

"That's probably not a bad idea," Jacky said, and Simon's eyes widened in surprise. "But don't go right away. Give yourself a chance to think things over."

Simon smiled, and Jacky saw Dante climb on the mechanical bull, but he kept his attention on Simon. "I figured you'd give me more of an argument," Simon said.

"Nope. You need to work things out with your family." Jacky smiled. "Besides, I'm going with you."

Simon began to cough, and Jacky's smile turned into a grin. "You're what?" Simon gasped.

"You're not going to face them alone, so I'm going to go with you. I can take care of myself, and I don't have a vested emotional interest in anyone except you."

"Jacky," Simon said once he'd caught his breath. "I need to do this alone."

"It's your turn," Dante said, and Simon stepped toward the machine. Jacky watched him climb on and then stared as he rode, hips rolling and arms swinging. The tension that had filled Simon all day seemed to drain away. He got thrown to the mat, rolled, and came up with a smile. Gardner climbed on, and Simon came over to stand next to Jacky once again.

"Feel better?" Jacky asked, and Simon nodded. "Good. Because you aren't going home alone."

"I won't be alone. Gardner will be there, and my family already knows him." Jacky growled softly, the sound rumbling in his throat. "What's that for?" Simon whispered.

"Nothing," Jacky said and turned in time to see Gardner get bucked off the machine. Dante took his turn, and then Simon was up again. "He looks really good," Jacky told Dante when he came over to stand beside him.

"He really does. Once this thing with his family has been settled, it'll probably be time for him to go on the road. There are a lot of rodeos, and he needs to be seen so he can snag a sponsor. That isn't going to happen unless he gets some exposure." Jacky nodded. He loved rodeo, and he loved that Simon loved it and was good at what he did. But he hated the thought of the traveling and separation. There was nothing he could do about it, though, and he certainly wasn't going to tell Simon. Simon needed support, and Jacky knew what the rodeo life was like.

"He's going back to his family to try to work things out," Jacky told Dante, who nodded slowly in that way he had when he was thinking.

"You said you'd go with him, and he told you no, didn't he?" Dante asked, and Jacky scowled.

"Would you quit with the mind-reader act?" Jacky said. Simon ended his ride as the machine slowed and came to a halt. "And yes, that's what he told me."

"Go again," Dante said to Simon. "And this time, start testing your balance. It's not enough to be able to stay on; you have to know how to recover when the balance gets a little wonky. There are lots of times when a small adjustment can give you that extra second you need."

Gardner turned on the machine, and Simon took another turn. Jacky watched and realized he was getting excited. There was nothing quite as sexy as seeing Simon in his hip-rolling, body-swaying element.

The guys took turns riding for a while. Jacky even took a few turns on a low setting. By the time they were done, Simon seemed to feel better and had some of his fire back, but it didn't last long. By evening, he was once again quiet and brooding. At dinner, he pushed his food around his plate and then disappeared outside. Gardner followed, but returned a few minutes later with a small shrug.

After dinner and evening chores, they all settled in the living room. Ryan showed Gardner the room he'd be using. They watched television, and every sound from outside made Jacky jump and look toward the door. Dante and Ryan eventually said good night. "He'll be fine," Ryan told him, and Jacky knew he was right, but he still worried.

"I'm sorry he isn't around," Gardner said.

"He's always been a bit of a loner. I never understood it before, but it makes sense now."

"At least it isn't me," Jacky said.

"No. He's always dealt with his problems on his own. It's just the way he is. I think he knew his family wouldn't understand him, so he either kept to himself or he'd spend time at our place. But I can tell you, it isn't you." Gardner shifted in the chair. "Frizz used to talk about horses and riding nonstop. But when we were talking this afternoon, he kept talking about you. So I'd say none of this has anything to do with you or how he feels about you."

"I know he's finding his way. It's something we all have to do." Jacky sighed. "I just wish I could help him. I've been through it already. I know how it feels."

"Did your family reject you?" Gardner asked.

Jacky shook his head. "Mine didn't, but Ryan's did." Jacky thought he heard footsteps on the porch, but when he listened closely, he didn't hear anything. "I'm sorry you came all this way to be ignored."

"It's okay. We talked, and he knows my family has his back, just like you guys do. That's why I came. I also didn't know he had such a tight group of people here. He told me how you all piled into the diner when he was meeting his dad. That's so cool." Gardner yawned. "I gotta go to bed. My dad is watching the ranch while I'm gone, but we're down a couple hands, so I gotta head back in the morning. I already told Frizz." Gardner stood up and yawned again. "Take care of him."

"We will," Jacky said and watched as Gardner ambled toward the hallway.

Jacky thought Gardner had come a long way for a very short visit, but then he realized he'd have done the exact same thing for Ryan. In fact, in a way he had during the mess with Ryan's coming out.

He tried staying up a while more, but his own fatigue got the better of him, and he went down the hall to his room. He suspected Simon had gone back to his room in the bunkhouse, and Jacky was more than a little disappointed. But if Simon wanted space, then he'd give it to him. He got ready for bed and climbed beneath the covers. Jacky listened for a while for the sound of booted feet coming down the hall, but heard nothing, and after a while he closed his eyes.

Jacky woke knowing he wasn't alone. The door was partially open, and he heard soft footsteps. Then the covers were lifted and Simon settled into bed next to him.

"Is this okay?" Simon asked, and Jacky pulled him close, guiding their mouths together. Jacky groaned softly at first, but it quickly increased in intensity as Simon slipped his hand down Jacky's hips, pushing his briefs down. Simon was already naked, and when their cocks slid against each other, Jacky moaned into Simon's mouth. His reward was to be kissed harder. He throbbed between their bodies, each of Simon's gentle touches sending a jolt of raw desire through him.

He shimmied out of his underwear and gripped Simon tight, slid his hands down his strong, smooth back, and cupped his butt for leverage, bucking up against him.

"Simon," Jacky whispered when they broke the kiss. Jacky could feel the energy pouring off him, and he reached for the kit on the nightstand and located a condom and a package of lube. He pressed them into Simon's hand and listened as the package ripped open. It was nearly completely dark, so instead of his eyes, Jacky used his hands and body. Simon shifted his weight, and Jacky stroked his shoulders before placing his legs on them. He was nearly bent in half as Simon pressed to him. Jacky cradled Simon's head, running his fingers through his soft hair and over his ears.

Jacky had felt Simon's kinetic urgency since he'd joined him in bed. He knew this wouldn't be gentle, and he was prepared for that. Thankfully, the condom was lubed. Jacky relaxed his muscles and pressed back against Simon until his body opened. He gasped softly as Simon continued pressing into him. No way would he ask him to stop. Occasionally Jacky liked things a little rough, and he knew that was what he was going to get this time. Simon vibrated with excitement as he slammed the final inch inside him. Jacky moaned, and then Simon held still for a few seconds before beginning to move.

It took Jacky a few seconds for his body to catch up to what Simon was doing to him. But when he did, he caught Simon's rhythm and moved with it. "That's it. Give me all you've got. Let go of everything and give it to me," Jacky whispered, and Simon slammed into him, quickly pulled out, and slammed into him again, the slap of flesh on flesh filling the room. "Jesus," Jacky gasped.

"Hurting?" Simon gasped.

"No. Don't you dare stop," Jacky moaned, throwing his head back as Simon pegged his gland again and again. "Jesus Christ," Jacky cried as his eyes rolled back in his head. Sweat ran down his cheeks and the bed shook. Jacky had been steadying himself by holding on to Simon, but now he grasped the bedding and held on as each thrust rippled through his body. He didn't have to see to know Simon was rolling his hips.

"You're the bull," Simon said, and Jacky chuckled for a brief second before the retort flew from his mind. He wouldn't be able to take much more of this, and sure enough, within seconds, Simon began stroking him hard and fast. Jacky gasped and left his pleasure in Simon's care. He could do nothing else. His body reacted, gravitating to whatever Simon wanted.

Within moments, Jacky could take no more and he gave up the last of his control. Openmouthed, in near disbelief, he plummeted over the edge of passion, taking Simon along with him.

Jacky floated for a few seconds and then wrapped his arms around Simon and tugged him close. They kissed softly, in total contrast to the near animalistic rutting from a few minutes before.

"I didn't hurt you, did I?" Simon asked.

"Hell, no," Jacky said. Their bodies separated, and he whimpered softly before stretching out his legs on the bedding. "It was what you needed, and I was happy to be part of it."

"You're sure?" Simon whispered, and Jacky gathered him tightly to him, stroking Simon's back. "We can make love that way whenever you need or want to." Jacky closed his eyes and sighed softly as Simon held him in return.

Eventually, Simon got off the bed and went into the bathroom. He must have taken care of the condom. He cleaned them up, and when he returned again, Jacky closed his eyes and clung to him. "Just so you know, I'm going with you."

"Jacky," Simon growled almost sinfully. Under different circumstances, that sound would be sexy as hell.

"Don't growl at me," Jacky said, rolling on his side.

"It won't help," Simon told him.

"You're not going alone, so either you can accept it or I'll find out when you're going and drive up myself. It won't be that hard to figure out where your family lives." Jacky cupped Simon's face in his hands. "You aren't going alone. So we can do this the easy way or the hard way. And for the record, you might be the cowboy, but don't try to outstubborn me. I'll kick your tight round cowboy butt all the way back here if you try to leave without me."

"Damn," Simon sighed, and Jacky smiled. "You really are a pain in the ass sometimes."

"No, actually, that's you, thinking you have to do everything alone. If you want to have a relationship with someone, then you need to let them help. It isn't all about you or me—it's about us." Jacky rolled over onto his back. "That is, if you want this to be a relationship and not us just messing around."

"Is that what happened before?" Simon asked.

"Pretty much," Jacky said. "So if that's what this is, then say so now and save both of us a lot of trouble and drama."

Simon sighed again. "It's not. It's more than that. I do love you. It's just that everything feels like its falling apart. I know I should have known this could happen, but how do you prepare for it?"

"You don't. You deal with it… and you let the people who care about you help." Jacky tugged Simon next to him and slowly rubbed his back. "It will be okay. I'm sure of it. I'll get out of work early on Friday, and we'll drive up."

"But what about… you know…. Where will we sleep?" Simon asked.

"We'll make a hotel reservation. That way we'll have a place separate from your family. You won't be expecting them to provide us a place to stay, and that will give you a place to go if you need to get away, or if things get too difficult."

"Okay. If they don't call by the end of the week, I'll call them and tell them what's happening, and we'll see how things go."

Simon was nervous, and it showed in the quaver in his voice. "I have no idea what kind of reception we'll get."

"I know that, and I'm sure you'll want to talk to your parents alone. That's fine. Just know I'll be there for you and you have someone on your side." Jacky tightened his hold on Simon and breathed a sigh of relief. Maybe what he'd feared wouldn't turn into reality. Simon wasn't Juan, thank God. Jacky closed his eyes and hoped against hope that Simon would be able to sleep. It wasn't long before Jacky's fatigue caught up with him and he nodded off. He wasn't a particularly deep sleeper, and when he woke and Simon was still in his arms, Jacky went right back to sleep. He had no doubt they would need the rest for the drama ahead.

THEY got up in time to say good-bye to Gardner, and after Simon finished his necessary Sunday chores, they spent the rest of the day together. Simon was subdued, but since he'd come up with a plan, he didn't seem nearly as depressed. In the early evening, Jacky packed and headed home. He spent the week working at the Western store, keeping busy. He and Simon talked on the phone each day at least once, and on Friday, Jacky left the shop at noon and managed to beat most of the traffic out of the city. He arrived at the ranch and parked next to Simon's truck, careful not to hit the door he'd left open. Jacky got his bag out of the trunk and stowed it behind the seat in the cab of Simon's truck before climbing the porch steps and heading inside.

The house was silent. Ryan would be at work, and Dante must have been out and about on the ranch. He went back outside, but didn't see or hear Simon. He wandered around a little and eventually found him in the shed, riding the mechanical bull for all he was worth while Dante watched. Jacky saw him ride the machine for a few seconds before Simon was thrown. The machine came to a stop, and Jacky stepped inside.

"I guess it's time for you to go," Dante observed and pulled Simon into a quick hug.

"I need to shower quick, and then we can go," Simon said.

"Okay. I'll meet you by the truck when you're ready," Jacky said. He was about to turn to leave when Simon stopped him with a hand on his shoulder. Jacky turned back around, and Simon leaned close and kissed him.

"You were right. I don't need to do this alone," Simon whispered and then kissed him again before pulling away. Simon walked toward the bunkhouse, and Jacky touched his tingling lips, controlling the urge to follow him. Instead, he consoled himself with the view of Simon's tight bubble butt, bobbing in those almost obscenely thin jeans. After a few seconds, Jacky blinked to pull his mind out of fantasies of just what he wanted to do with that rear end.

"He's quite something," Dante said from behind him.

"You can say that again." Jacky agreed, still watching Simon.

"He's a natural rider with a great rhythm. If he can get his mind back on riding, he'll be one hell of a contender. Jacky, are you listening?" Dante asked with a chuckle.

"I agree with you. Simon is one hell of a rider," Jacky said, remembering the last time they were together. He shifted slightly and hoped Dante didn't notice.

"God, you're hopeless," Dante said.

"Hey, a dirty mind is a terrible thing to waste," Jacky quipped as he turned toward Dante, and they shared a laugh as Dante closed up the shed. The two of them walked back to the house together. Jacky noticed that Simon's truck door was still open, so he closed it. Simon's attention must have been pretty scattered that morning.

He waited on the porch until Simon came out of the bunkhouse carrying a small bag. Jacky joined him at the truck while Simon stowed the last of his gear. They said good-bye to Dante and the guys before getting in the truck and pulling out.

The drive was miles and miles of next to nothing to see—flat, open land broken up only by a few trees and the occasional town. He and Jacky took turns driving because it was so boring and there was nothing to look at. They crossed the border into Oklahoma and continued driving. The land looked pretty much the same. They stopped in a small town and ate at a greasy spoon before continuing on. About an hour before sunset, he pulled off the freeway and continued north.

There was just enough light to see the house and grounds when Simon turned onto a long driveway and approached a large red-brick house with white columns. "This is where you live?"

"Where my parents live, yes," Simon said. He pulled up to the house and parked. Jacky waited to see if anyone came out. They got out of the truck, and the front door opened. A group of kids raced out and over to Simon, a little girl in a pink dress bringing up the rear. Simon hugged each of them and lifted the little girl into the air.

"How's my big girl?" Simon asked her, and she squealed in delight as Simon spun her around.

"Simon," his father said as he came down the walk, and Jacky knew the instant he saw him. "You brought a…." He swallowed. "Friend?"

"Dad, this is Jacky. Jacky, this is my father, Isaac," Simon said, without elaborating, and his dad came forward and they shook hands. Simon set the little girl on her feet and walked to where a middle-aged woman stood on the steps. Simon hugged her, and Jacky noticed she returned it. At least that was hopeful. But the tension in the air felt like an electrical storm was brewing at any moment, even though the sky was clear as a bell.

"Mom, this is Jacky," Simon said when he stepped away, and Jacky shook her hand.

"I'm Miriam, I'm three," the little girl said, and she lifted her arms to be picked up. Jacky picked her up—she obviously wasn't shy at all. "Will you take me on a horsey ride?"

Jacky looked to Simon, who said, "Yes, while I'm here we can go for a ride."

Apparently this was a big deal, because the energy of the other kids ramped up. Simon was obviously trying to act like things were normal, but by the way his mom and dad were exchanging looks, everything was far from normal for them. Jacky half expected one of them to take Miriam from his arms, but they seemed content to watch him. "Let Simon and his friend come inside," Simon's mother said, and the kids dispersed, but Miriam seemed content to let him carry her, at least until they were inside, and then he put her down and she took off after the others.

"Hey, no fair, I'm little," she said as she ran into one of the rooms to catch up with the other kids.

Jacky stood next to Simon in the large entrance hall, feeling the nervous energy rolling off him. Jacky was nervous as well, but reminded himself he was here to support Simon and his nerves weren't anywhere near as important as being there for Simon.

"Let's go into the living room," Simon's mother said.

Simon glanced at him and then let his parents lead the way. They moved into a formal room that obviously hadn't seen much use in a house full of children. The light-colored furniture was pristine and the glass tables showed nary a fingerprint. Jacky sat at the end of the sofa, at a reasonable distance from Simon.

"When you called, you said you wanted to talk," Simon's father said. Obviously he was someone who got down the business. "I assume Jack knows why you're here."

"Isaac, there's no need to be rude," Simon's mother said softly and pulled a tissue from her sleeve. "Son," his mother began, "we just don't understand."

"I know you don't, Mom, and I don't fully understand either." Simon shifted until he was perched on the edge of the sofa. "I'm sorry you found out the way you did. I should have been the one to tell you. But I can't change facts."

"Yes, you can," his father said. "I found a place where they can cure you."

"No, they can't," Simon said. "They only tell you what you want to hear, and I'm not going to be anyone's guinea pig. I told you that before you left."

"Then we don't have anything to say to each other," his father said, standing up.

"So that's how it is," Simon said, standing up as well, staring at his father. "You make some pronouncement, and that's the end of it. I always thought you were about family." Simon's voice was firm but urgent. "Didn't you tell all of us that there was nothing we could do that would make you stop loving us? Well, your parental love is being tested—are you going to pass or fail?" Simon pointed toward the other room. "What if Miriam brings home a girlfriend instead of a boyfriend? What if Jeremiah decides he wants move to Tibet and become a Buddhist monk? Are you going to stop loving them? Or is this a special punishment because I'm gay?" Simon whirled around. "Come on, Jacky, I think we're done. Coming here was a mistake."

"Simon," his mother said softly, and he stopped. Jacky watched as Simon's anger turned to hurt. "We don't understand, but you're still our son." Simon nodded and then turned and left the room. Jacky followed Simon as he strode across the hall toward the front door. "Simon."

They both stopped as Simon's mother walked toward them. "I won't pretend to understand all this, because I don't and I doubt I ever will. But will you be back tomorrow?" Simon's father walked around them and went into a different room, then closed the door.

"Sure, Mom," Simon said and then forced a smile before leaving the house. He closed the door behind them and strode to the truck. He walked around to the passenger seat and climbed in. Obviously he wanted Jacky to drive, so Jacky climbed in, and Simon handed him the keys.

Jacky programmed the GPS with the name of the hotel he'd booked and followed the vocal directions.

"It's okay, Simon. You weren't expecting this to be easy. And your mother didn't want you to go. She's trying, but they're both having a hard time."

"But…."

"But nothing. I loved the way you spoke to your dad. He impresses me as the type of person who responds to respect, and he isn't going to respect someone who agrees with him all the time. He might not like it, but he'll respect your strength."

"Maybe this was a bad idea," Simon whispered.

"No, it was a good idea. They need to see you're the same person they always knew and you still like the same things. So go riding tomorrow, do things with your brothers and sisters like you always did. Have fun, and don't worry about your mom and dad. They love you."

Simon nodded and then turned to stare out the window into the blackness. He said nothing, and Jacky continued driving until they pulled into the hotel parking lot. Thankfully, it was a decent chain hotel, not large, but predictable. "Let's go on inside and get checked in. Then we can get something to eat before going to bed."

Simon nodded blankly and got out of the car. "I'm sorry," he said as he grabbed his bag. "I don't know what I was expecting."

"Expect nothing. You're here because you're willing to make an effort. It looks like your mother is willing to make one too. That's a win." Jacky grabbed his bag, and they walked across the parking lot and into the hotel. Jacky checked in and got the key cards. Then they walked together down the hall to their room. Of course, they found two double beds. That hadn't been Jacky's reservation, but he wouldn't make a scene. They set down their stuff, left the room, and found a restaurant for a quick dinner before returning and getting ready for bed. "It's going to be okay."

"I wish I could be as optimistic," Simon said as he got into bed, and Jacky held him close, hoping like hell he was right.

# CHAPTER EIGHT

THE visit to his parents was not at all what he'd hoped. Simon's father either gave him the silent treatment or simply stayed away for most of the time he was there. His mother tried, but seemed to ignore the reason he'd come, so every time he tried to speak with her, she either changed the subject or found something that urgently needed to be done. He did take the kids riding with Jacky, and they had a ball. For a while things were almost like they'd been before his entire world had changed. Miriam rode with him, and the boys teased each other back and forth, with the younger kids just happy to be on their ponies. Even Solomon got to ride his pony all by himself, under Simon's watchful eye. His mother made a nice dinner Saturday night, and thankfully the kids didn't seem aware of the tension around the table. They ate and talked like nothing was different. After dinner, Simon made one more attempt to talk to his father. All he received was near stony silence, and he gave up. He and Jacky went back to the hotel, and Simon figured that was that. His family might come around in time, but it was obviously going to take a while.

The following morning, they left for the ranch from the hotel. Simon wasn't happy with how they'd left things, but he'd tried, and that was all he could do. He couldn't change his father's mind. That had to come from him. They arrived at the ranch late in the afternoon, and Jacky said he'd get up early to drive into the city. They spent the night together, making love quietly. Simon needed reassurance, and Jacky gave it to him with every quiet moan and whimper. Afterward, they lay together and quickly fell asleep. Simon woke when Jacky got out of bed. They cleaned up, and Simon saw Jacky off before starting on his chores.

The entire week, Simon got up early and worked until almost sunset. It kept his mind occupied. When he wasn't working, he spent time on the mechanical bull, mastering his technique and taking out his frustrations on the machine. By the time the weekend came around again, Simon felt better and had started to understand that his life and relationship with his family was never going to be the same. He did call his parents, but only his mother would speak to him. They talked about superficial things, with her telling him about the antics of his siblings, and he talked to her about what he was doing on the ranch.

"Is Jacky coming?" Dante asked once chores were completed for the day.

"He said he was," Simon answered as they walked together toward the barn. "Are we training tonight?"

"No. You're riding in the morning, remember? I don't want you too tired, because these are supposed to be some highly ranked bulls. We'll see how they stack up, but you need to be ready for anything."

Simon nodded and turned as he heard tires on the gravel drive. Jacky's car pulled closer and stopped in its usual spot. Simon smiled as Jacky got out and walked right over to where he and Dante stood, carrying plastic bags in each hand. "What's all this?" Dante asked as Jacky walked up to Simon. They kissed gently, but the brief taste instantly lit a fire that sent heat all through Simon's body.

"I brought stuff to make dinner. Lord knows Ryan can't cook, and you two are practically helpless in the kitchen, so I figured I'd bring the stuff for a nice dinner tomorrow. Besides, I'm always here to visit, so I thought I'd help." Jacky headed inside, and Simon watched his backside swing slowly as he went.

"Damn, you two are a couple of hound dogs. He was watching you the same way last week," Dante commented, and Simon smiled.

"Look who's talking. I think around this place, ass-watching could be raised to an Olympic sport. In case you haven't noticed, neither you nor Ryan can take your eyes off each other either." Simon watched Jacky until he entered the house. Then he turned toward the barn. "I've got a few horses I need to look in on before I'm done for the day."

"All right," Dante said and headed toward the house. Simon strode into the barn and checked the legs of a few of the horses that Bob had questions about. They seemed fine to him, but Simon made a note to check on them again in the morning. Horses were strong *and* fragile creatures. They could run fast, but that same strength was the source of their weakness as well, so they had to be cared for and watched carefully. Seeing all was well. Simon made a final check on water and feed before he closed the barn doors and walked across the yard. Other horses were out in their paddocks, running or just standing, looking around. Simon had always thought horses were curious creatures. He walked up to the nearest paddock and leaned against the fence. After a few minutes, he heard Jacky approaching from behind. "How was your week?" he asked quietly.

"Good. Busy," Jacky answered and then stood next to him. "How was yours?"

"Busy trying not to worry and think about things," Simon answered honestly. "I keep thinking that I could make a difference if I went home to stay for a while." Simon saw Jacky's expression fall. He'd been torn all week about returning home to deal with things, and every time he thought about it, his heart ached at the thought of being away from Jacky.

"Did you call home?" Jacky whispered.

"Yes. But it didn't do any good," Simon told him. "And after I talk to them, I realize going home probably wouldn't help either. Sometimes I'm so confused I don't know which way to turn. They mean a lot to me, and then so do you, and…." Simon trailed off. "Anyway, like I said, I called, but nothing changed."

Jacky sighed softly. "They aren't going to change their minds overnight. All you can do is continue to be their son and eventually they'll come around." Jacky inhaled deeply and then turned to him with a smile. "Let me ask you this: Has how you feel about them changed? I mean really changed?"

"I guess not," Simon answered. "I still feel the same about them. I knew this was going to be hard for them to accept, so I shouldn't be shocked. I guess I'm disappointed."

"Then treat them the same way and forget the rest. Maybe if you act as though things haven't really changed, they'll eventually realize it too. So, if you used to call every couple of days, continue to do the same thing. Let them know that in ways that are important, you're the same."

"But who I love is important," Simon said, turning to look at Jacky. "And my dad hates me."

"I don't think so," Jacky said, bumping Simon's arm. "But I'll let you in on a secret. It takes a lot of energy for anyone to remain that disappointed and angry at someone. I suspect over time he'll cool down and start to realize you have to live your own life." Jacky bumped him again. "Your dad is used to taking care of you and the rest of the family. And to make things more difficult, your dad truly believes being gay is wrong. It's what he's been taught his entire life. That opinion isn't going to change quickly, but it can evolve over time." Jacky paused for a few seconds. "My mom was great when I came out, but her sister, Aunt Louise, was completely different. She's older than my mother, and of course when I came out, my mother talked to her. It wasn't pretty. Mom said Aunt Louise was a lot like your dad, and she even told my mother than I needed to see a psychologist or be committed to an asylum."

"That's pretty extreme," Simon said, his eyes widening.

"My mom told me she'd been looking for support when she'd talked to Aunt Louise and had no idea how vitriolic she'd be." Jacky actually chuckled. "The thing was, that Christmas we were supposed to go to Aunt Louise's for dinner."

"What happened?"

"Nothing. I played games with my cousins like I normally did, and we yelled and screamed like always. I hugged her the same way I always did when I saw her. Everything was normal. She saw I hadn't grown an extra head or a third eye. I didn't know about all the vitriol because she never acted that way around me. It wasn't until my mother told me about it a few years later that I even learned about it. Aunt Louise changed her mind because she got to know me as a gay person, but it happened over time. Eventually we were able to have a frank talk about it, but not until she was ready. Until then, it was a subject she'd ignore."

"Yeah. I'm getting plenty of that," Simon agreed.

"Then give them time," Jacky said.

Simon sighed and watched Hubble as he threw his head up and down before wandering over to where Simon stood. Simon stroked his chestnut neck. "I know everyone must be getting tired of me running on about this all the time." Simon turned to Jacky. "Frankly, I'm tired of it too. My parents—they'll act the way they want, and I can't do a fucking thing about it, but I'm letting it ruin everything else."

"So what are you going to do?"

"Get on with my life," Simon said resolutely. "I'm tired of whining and talking about it all the time. This is their problem, not mine. They're in another state, and all I'm doing is acting like a moping child." Simon let go of Hubble, and he wandered away. "Let's go inside and have some dinner. Maybe afterwards we can go into town for a drink and some fun. I'm tired of waiting around for something that might never happen." Simon took Jacky's hand, and they walked together toward the house.

Inside, Simon helped with dinner, and after everything had been cleaned up, Dante rounded up the other guys who wanted to go into town and they piled into trucks and caravanned to the local bar. Once inside, some headed for the bar while others grabbed tables. Drinks flowed, except for Ryan and one of the men, who were the designated drivers, and the conversation ran right along with it.

"I heard you're going over to Peterson's tomorrow to check out his bulls," Gus, one of the younger hands, said and then sucked the beer foam out of his bushy mustache. "I heard they're really something. Hoping for a high rank." Gus took another gulp. "You sure you're up to them?" he asked, and Gene, sitting next to him, elbowed him in the side. "Hey," Gus said as he nearly spilled some of his beer. "I didn't mean nothin' by it other than I don't want him getting hurt. Sheesh."

"He'll be fine," Dante said. "I've seen 'em, and yeah, those bulls will be ranked someday, but Frizz can handle them. He's the rodeo cowboy in residence now." Dante raised his mug slightly and then drank. Simon glanced at Jacky, who seemed nervous for a second, but then the expression vanished.

Simon watched how much he drank and limited himself to two beers. He had to ride the following day and didn't need any distractions. Jacky seemed to be doing the same. They spent a few hours there, listening to the band and watching people before Ryan signaled he was ready to go back. Those who were going with Ryan hopped into the truck, including Simon and Jacky, and they headed back. Simon held Jacky close in the cramped backseat area and did his best not to move too much while they rode back. Thankfully it wasn't too long before they pulled into the drive.

After they arrived, they piled out and unfolded themselves from the cramped backseat and made their way inside. They all settled in the living room and took turns yawning. It wasn't particularly late, but they all seemed talked out, so instead of sitting for long, Dante and Ryan headed off to bed, leaving them alone. Jacky moved closer and settled next to Simon, resting his head against his shoulder.

"You're been so wonderful," Simon whispered. "When I met you, I never expected all this to happen, and I keep waiting for you to figure out all this drama isn't worth it."

Jacky held him closer. "Of course you're worth it."

Simon stroked Jacky's hair. "When I first met you, I thought you'd only gone with me because I was a cowboy."

Jacky blushed slightly. "That was part of it at first, but it wasn't all of it. I will admit I never really expected to see you again, but I'm so glad I did." Jacky hugged him closer. "I looked a long time for someone like you." Jacky angled his head upward, and Simon kissed him. Then he shifted his weight on the sofa and deepened the kiss. Jacky moaned softly, and it took Simon a few seconds to remember where they were. He slowly got up off the sofa and tugged Jacky to his feet. Then, after turning out the lights, he led Jacky down the hall to the guest room and closed the door.

Simon stepped back and gazed at Jacky for a few seconds before pulling him into his arms. Jacky tilted his face up, and Simon took that as an invitation and kissed him hard, sucking lightly on his upper lip before slipping his tongue between Jacky's lips and feasting on his mouth. Jacky quivered in his arms and his little moans filled the room. Simon loved those sounds, and they spurred him on.

Slowly, he lifted Jacky off his feet, moved toward the bed, and pressed him back on the mattress. Simon tried to remove Jacky's clothes, but it wasn't working, so he stepped back and stripped off his own shirt and pants while Jacky did the same. Within seconds, they were both naked and Jacky was in his arms again, skin to skin. Perfection, absolute perfection, and nowhere else he'd rather be. They took their time, exploring, touching, and tasting. Simon found a spot at the base of Jacky's hip where if he licked it just so, Jacky would make the most deliciously needy little sound. It was amazing to be able to take his time and learn every inch of Jacky's body, discover what he liked, and especially what made him whimper with need. Simon was learning there was an art to making love, and part of that was to see how long he could keep Jacky on the whimpering, moaning, pleading edge of release. Tonight, he held them both on the precipice until they tumbled over together in a breath-gasping wet tangle.

After their release, Simon managed to get out of bed and grab a cloth to clean them up before returning and falling almost immediately asleep. He didn't wake until he heard others moving around in the house. "Jacky," he whispered, and his bedmate rolled over and clung to him, whimpering something about being quiet and then went back to sleep. "I need to get up. I have chores I need to finish, and then I'm supposed to try out some bulls."

"What time is it?" Jacky asked, snuggling closer without opening his eyes.

"Five thirty," Simon answered.

Jacky groaned. "Can't chores wait until the horses are awake?" Jacky rolled over, and Simon got out of bed. "Where are you going?" Jacky snuffled. "You kept me up half the night and now you're leaving. Not that I'm complaining about the being kept up part, just the leaving part." Jacky opened his eyes, reached out and caught his arm, then pulled Simon back. "Is anyone else even up?"

Simon chuckled. "I have things I have to do." He leaned over the bed. "You sleep for a while, and I'll come back when I'm done." Simon kissed Jacky lightly, and he settled back under the covers and closed his eyes. Simon stepped back and watched Jacky snooze for a few seconds before dressing quickly and grabbing shoes and socks. Then he left the room and finished getting ready in the living room before heading out to the barn.

The horses perked up when he came in, and Simon let those he could out into the pastures. He fed and watered the rest and checked the legs of the ones he'd looked in on the evening before. They were all fine, and Simon breathed a sigh of relief. He left the barn and met some of the guys in the yard. They were all yawning and seemed a bit slow because of the previous night. They piled into the trucks or onto ATVs and headed out to check on the cattle. Simon made the rounds of the horses in the pastures to make sure they were okay and all had water. Then he walked back to the house to see if Jacky was up. He wasn't, but the entire place smelled wonderfully of coffee. He found Ryan in the kitchen and poured himself a mug of wake-up juice before pouring a second and carrying it down the hall to Jacky's room.

It was still dark in the room, and Jacky didn't stir when he came in. Simon set the mugs on the nightstand and leaned over Jacky's sleeping form. "I brought you some coffee," Simon whispered. "We need to get up and going. Apparently Mr. Peterson is expecting us in an hour or so."

"Doesn't anyone around here ever sleep in like civilized people?" Jacky muttered as he rolled over. Simon handed him a mug, and he sat up, the thin covers pooling in his lap. The sight of Jacky's bare chest and sleepy eyes was damned tempting. He looked delectable, especially with that bit of hip showing. Simon wanted to put his mug back on the nightstand, lean over the bed, and see if he could lick those sexy little sounds out of Jacky again.

A soft knock sounded on the door. "Guys, you need to get moving. Peterson just called and he'll be looking for us in about an hour," Dante said.

Simon pushed his amorous thoughts from his mind and sat down in the chair in the corner.

"Don't you need to get ready?" Jacky asked, sipping from his mug.

"I have time to watch you," Simon said and waited for Jacky to crawl out from under the covers and walk over to him. "Now that's a world-class view," he whispered as a lump formed in his throat. "You're amazing." He set the mug on the floor by the chair and gently tugged Jacky closer. Then Simon took Jacky's mug and placed it next to his before gathering a beautifully naked Jacky into his arms. Jacky's warm skin passed under his hands, and he stroked down Jacky's back and then down and over the curve of his butt. He so badly wanted to carry him back to the bed and forget about the other things he needed to do. Jacky was so very tempting.

"Come on, cowboy," Jacky whispered once they broke their kiss. "I need to get dressed, and you need to get your things together so you can teach these bulls a thing or two." Jacky pulled away and picked up his coffee mug before grabbing his bag and disappearing into the bathroom. Simon took a deep breath and then let it out slowly, trying to calm his quickly beating heart. He was a lucky man and he knew it. Jacky was special, and Simon smiled at the thought that Jacky loved him.

After a few minutes he heard the shower start and was tempted to join Jacky, but instead Simon left the bedroom and hurried outside and across the yard to the bunkhouse, where he kept his gear.

The bunkhouse was quiet, since the guys were out working, and he went right to his room and made sure everything was in his bag. Then he cleaned up and changed before slinging the bag over his shoulder and heading out to his truck. By the time Simon was ready to go, Jacky stood yawning on the porch with his mug in his hand. He looked cute, almost like a sleepy little boy with his hair going in every direction, eyes half closed. "Come on, let's get ready to go," Dante said excitedly, jogging past Jacky and down the porch steps. "We'll take two trucks," he said as he continued toward his. "Jacky, let's go. Ryan, you need to hurry up."

"How can you be so chipper at this ungodly hour of the morning?" Ryan groused as he came out of the house. "It's Saturday, for God's sake. Let me sleep in for another hour."

"Amen," Jacky echoed, and the two sleepyheads walked toward the trucks. Jacky pulled open the passenger door of Simon's truck and climbed in, then put on his seat belt and slumped in the seat without moving except to sip from his mug. Simon got in as well and started the engine. "Don't spill," he said softly, and Jacky growled. Then Jacky finished his coffee and wedged the mug into one of the cup holders. "You could have stayed at the house."

"I'm fine. I just need a chance to wake up," Jacky muttered. Simon backed out of his spot and followed Dante down the drive. The ride to the Peterson place took about ten minutes, and by the time they arrived, Jacky was awake, alert, and looking around at everything. "Cool place," he said, and Simon had to agree as they pulled in and parked. Horses ran in paddocks, and as soon as he got out, Simon heard bulls snorting and grunting nearby. There was something about that sound that instantly got his blood racing, and excitement coursed through him.

"Dante," a middle-aged man called as he came over to meet them. "Glad you could make it."

"John, this is Frizz. He's a talented rider. Won his first buckle just a while ago, and he'll be trying out your bulls."

"It's a pleasure to meet you," Simon said, shaking hands.

"Not to cast doubt on your abilities, young man, but these are bulls I hope will be ranked for national competition. There are no money bulls here." He turned to Dante, who nodded.

"Frizz not only rode, but spurred Widowmaker," Dante said, and Mr. Peterson's eyebrows lifted.

"That was you? I thought that was only a rumor." Mr. Peterson whistled. "Okay, then, let's get you ready. I'll have the handlers ready and the boys set to distract the bulls. Give us fifteen minutes and we'll be ready for you," he said before hurrying off.

"With this place so close, why don't we practice on real bulls?" Simon asked Dante. "At least once in a while."

"Because of the danger. The machine is more forgiving. Also, we'd wear the bulls out with the number of rides we need to train." Dante wiped his brow. "Get yourself ready. Don't make the man wait."

Simon grabbed his bag and set it on the ground. He stepped into his chaps and pulled on his vest. He also grabbed his riding boots from the back of the truck as well as his helmet. Once he was dressed and ready, he threw what he didn't need in the back of the truck and slung his bull rope over his shoulder before following Dante around to the chute. Simon was so excited, he barely felt the dry ground beneath his feet. Peterson's men were loading the first of the bulls into the chute, and Simon turned to Jacky and grinned. There was none of the nervousness he'd felt during competition. This was simply riding, something he loved to do.

"Focus," Dante told him.

"I am," Simon said.

"No, you're not. Every time you get on the back of a bull, you have to focus just like you do in competition. No one is going to score your ride, and there's no crowd, but that doesn't matter. The bull is just as fierce and dangerous." Dante's serious expression snapped the reverie from Simon's mind.

He nodded and watched as the men loaded the bull. It snorted something fierce. "We just clipped his horns a few days ago, and he's still sore about it," one of the handlers said. "This is Gorgon," he said they closed the back gate, locking the bull in the chute. He continued snorting as Simon climbed the fence and the men got his bull rope in place. Then Simon settled on Gorgon's back. The bull's power radiated up through his ass and balls. He had no doubt this bull had one hell of a ride in store for him. Simon made sure he was ready and lifted his arm over his head.

"Ready," he cried, and the front gate opened. Gorgon leaped forward, but Simon was ready for him. "Hell, yes!" Simon cried and went with Gorgon's spin. He spurred him, and Gorgon spun faster, determined to sink him in the well. Simon compensated, and damned if the fucker didn't stop and spin the other way. Simon compensated partially and then spurred him hard. Gorgon leaped almost straight up and then pounded into the ground, the shock reverberating through Simon's body. The next leap sent Simon flying off Gorgon's back, and he used what little leverage he had to push away from the bull. He landed, rolled, and scrambled to the fence while the other men called out and distracted the mean son of a bitch.

The guys cheered, and Simon wasn't sure if they were cheering for him or the bull. "Almost nine seconds," Dante told him. "That was a hell of a ride." Dante clapped him on the back, and Jacky beamed at Simon as he walked to where the men were gathering. Gorgon was herded out of the ring, and Peterson clapped him on the shoulder.

"That was quite a display," he said.

"Gorgon's one fucking awesome bull. You'll have no trouble getting him ranked," Simon told him. "Damn thing loves to go for the well."

"You were certainly ready for him," Peterson said.

"Just lucky, I guess," Simon told him. The truth was, he'd had a feeling that was what the bull was going to do, but he didn't know how he knew—he just did.

"There was no luck involved," Mr. Peterson said. "The men are going to get Disorganized Chaos ready, if you're okay to go again. It'll be about half an hour, so take a breather."

Simon nodded and joined Jacky while he waited for the next bull.

"Are you okay? You didn't get hurt, did you? Does your arm ache?" Jacky fussed.

Simon smiled at him. "I'm fine. I got flipped around, but nothing hurts."

"Okay," Jacky said, looking at him strangely, like he wasn't sure if he should believe Simon or not. "You'd tell me if it did, right?"

"Stop worrying. I'm fine," Simon said with a smile and watched as the men worked to wrangle the next bull.

"Two is enough for today," Mr. Peterson said after striding over. "It would be great if you could come over next weekend and ride Torrential Downpour." He smiled. "I know. I didn't name them. Believe it or not, my wife did, and she has a curious sense of humor."

"That would be fine," Simon said and turned back to watch them work with Disorganized Chaos. He seemed to go into the chute okay, but Dante had told him some fought it and others didn't care about the chute; they only got ornery as soon as a rider sat on their back. Simon waited until the men signaled they were ready and then walked over to the chute. Once the bull rope was in place, he climbed on, and instantly Chaos tensed and snorted. This bull sure hated to be ridden. Simon got into position and signaled. The chute opened, and Chaos raced out, pulled to a stop, and jumped into the air, twirling as he did. Damn, Simon felt his teeth rattle and his spine twist with that one. He held on and managed to correct his balance a little, but by then Chaos was already whipping around the other way. Simon felt the grip of his legs slip and then he was thrown upward. He let go of the rope and flew through the air, then landed hard on the ground. He saw the sky for a brief second and then that was all he remembered for a few seconds.

His mind told him to move, so Simon got up, cracked his eyes open, and headed to the fence. He could feel the ground rumble beneath his feet. He leaped for the fence and fumbled over it, fell to the other side and then lay still. Everything hurt, and he had no idea what was wrong. All he knew was that breathing was difficult, and when he opened his eyes, the world seemed to spin. So he kept them closed and listened as multiple voices talked around him.

"I'm okay," Simon said softly, even though his mind was like swirled pudding, and when he tried to move, he was held down.

"I'm calling an ambulance," Ryan said, and Simon felt someone take his hand. He figured it was Jacky.

"I'm okay, just give me a minute," Simon said, and then he blacked out.

He remembered being moved and then swaying back and forth. He heard voices, but they felt far away at first, moving closer and then falling away. He tried to concentrate on something, but then gave up and let his mind float. After a while he was moved again, and lights flashed behind his eyes.

"Simon, it's me," Jacky said softly. Simon felt someone take his hand, and he swam upward through the clouds surrounding his mind and opened his eyes. "Simon."

"What happened?" he asked. The room was dimly lit, and Simon glanced around. He was in a hospital room. When he turned toward the window, he saw it was dark. "How long have I been here?"

"You blacked out and have a concussion," Jacky told him. "But you're going to be fine." Jacky smiled at him. "You've been in the hospital for most of the day. How do you feel?"

"My head aches, but other than that I feel okay. Did I break anything?"

"No bones," Jacky said. "You just hit your head. The doctor said your helmet probably saved your life. We've been waiting for you to wake up for hours." Simon looked around again, afraid to move his head.

"Who's we?" he asked, and his question was answered when his mother and father walked into the room. His mother gasped and then hurried to the bed. "I'm going to be fine, Mom."

"When Jacky called us and told us what happened, we hurried down," she said, wiping at the corner of her eyes. She moved to the opposite side of his bed and gently stroked his hand. "We had to come," she said and then swallowed hard, looking over at his father, who nodded. "Jacky said you had fallen and hadn't woken up. So we got here as fast as we could." She leaned over the bed and kissed his cheek.

"Why? I thought…."

"We were wrong, sweetheart," she said. "We understand that now." She turned away and began sobbing softly.

"Simon, we still don't understand everything, and it may take your mother and me some time, but that doesn't mean we don't want you in our lives or in the lives of your brothers and sisters. You're still our son, and it's going to take some adjusting for us to know… to understand… that, well, we have a gay son," his father whispered.

"It's not the end of the world, Dad," Simon said softly. "For a long time I thought it was, but Jacky showed me that I can be gay and be loved." He held Jacky's hand. "He loves me, Dad, and that's what counts. See, I think I figured it out. It's all about the love. That's what you always taught all of us." Simon slowly rolled his head on the pillow. "I love him, and he loves me, and I believe that makes God happy." Simon smiled at Jacky and got a smile back. His mother cleared her throat nervously. "Anyway, I'm glad you're here." Simon didn't let go of Jacky's hand.

"You gave us quite a scare," his father said, and he stepped closer to the bed. Jacky patted Simon's hand and moved away. After a quick look that Simon returned, Jacky left the room. A few minutes later he returned with one of the nurses. She scooted everyone out of the room and checked Simon over. She placed a thermometer device against his temple, and it beeped. Then she took his pulse and blood pressure.

"You seem better, sugar," she said with a smile. "I'll call the doctor, so he can take a look at you as well." She straightened his bedding and fluffed his pillow. "Do you need anything for pain?"

"No," Simon answered. She smiled at him again and pulled the curtain back before leaving the room. Jacky moved next to him once again, and Simon's parents watched them nervously. "Where are Dante and Ryan?"

"They had to get back to the ranch, but they'll come by a little later," Jacky told him.

"That's good," Simon said and closed his eyes. He was tired, and the room was dark and quiet. He must have dozed off, because he woke when the doctor came in.

"It's good to see you awake," he said and took out a light, then shone it into Simon's eyes. "You're very lucky. I need to run some tests to make sure there's no permanent damage, but you should be fine. I'll schedule the tests for the morning, and we'll want to keep an eye on you for a few days, but barring something unexpected, you should be able to go home in a day or two."

"Thank you, Doctor," Simon's father said, and his mother nodded and dabbed her eyes.

The doctor nodded to all of them before leaving the room. "Thank goodness," his mother said. "You're going to be fine, and in a few days you can come home."

"I'm going back to the ranch," Simon said, and his mother turned to his father.

"Son, you were knocked out with a concussion. Surely that's taught you this rodeo business is dangerous. You weren't even riding in competition and you could have been killed. So we thought it was time for you to give this up and come on home."

"No, Dad. I'm still gonna ride, and I'm staying at the ranch. It's my home now. I have a job I like with people I like working with. I also get to ride and compete." Simon slowly sat up. His head ached a little, but the room stayed still. "This is what I want, Dad, and it hasn't changed." Simon looked at his dad and then turned to his mother. "I'm an adult now, and it's time I take care of myself. You and Mom did a good job raising me, and I appreciate everything you've done for me, but it's time I was on my own."

His mother sniffled softly, but it was his father who stepped closer and nodded. "Like I said, I don't understand this gay thing, but I do understand you growing up to be your own man, and we can respect that." He touched Simon's shoulder. "That doesn't mean your mother and I won't worry about you. Because you know how your mother feels about this rodeo stuff, but you're a man now and you need to make your own decisions." He turned around. "Come on, Martha, let's let Simon rest for a while." He placed his arm around her shoulder. "We'll come back to see him in the morning, and you can fuss over him then."

His mother walked up to the bed and kissed Simon lightly on the forehead. "I don't understand any of this, but I'll try," she said and kissed him again before straightening up and wiping her eyes. Then she and his dad said good night and left the room.

"I can't believe they came," Simon said.

"Of course they did. When they were taking you to the hospital, I followed behind with Dante and Ryan and called them right away. They're your parents and they needed to know. What I didn't expect was for your dad to somehow get hold of a helicopter. They got here in a few hours and landed on the roof of one of the buildings nearby."

"They came by helicopter?" Simon asked, his head spinning a little, and not from his injury.

"Yes. They really do care. They're having a hard time understanding things, but when you were hurt, I think what was really important came into focus, and it didn't matter if you were gay. All that counted was that their son was hurt."

Simon closed his eyes, not knowing what to say. "Thank you," he said softly.

"Hey, I didn't do anything. They're your folks—it's what they do. I don't expect to be getting any invitations to a family dinner soon, but maybe they don't think I have two heads anymore." Jacky chuckled and settled into the chair by the bed. "Now go on and get some rest."

"I would, but I'm hungry," Simon said.

"I'll call down to see if I can get you something," Jacky said. He stood up and walked around to where the phone sat on the tray.

Simon reached out and caught his arm. "I love you, Jacky. I know this had to be a worry for you too, but I want you to know that I love you."

"I love you too." Jacky leaned over the bed and kissed him.

"I thought you'd be too tired for that," Dante said as he and Ryan entered the room. "You must be feeling better."

"I am," Simon said. He really was. He had Jacky, his family, and close friends who cared about him and supported him. What more could he want? Jacky called for some food and then sat on the edge of the bed. Simon carefully pulled him close and closed his eyes. He had everything he always wanted. Well, almost everything, but he had what was important. "I love you," he mumbled and tugged Jacky closer with a smile on his face.

# EPILOGUE

*Three months later*

SIMON shifted nervously yet again as he watched the bronc busting. Gardner had done well and was right near the top of the standings. All he needed was a really good ride and he could take over the lead. Simon listened as Gardner was announced and watched him wave his hat before getting situated. Then the gate opened and the horse burst into the arena with Gardner on his back. He looked good, keeping in control. When the buzzer sounded, Gardner bailed and landed on his feet, then ran toward the rail while the clowns distracted the calming horse. Gardner waved his hat from the rail, and Simon knew that had been enough. The scores confirmed it, and Simon jumped to his feet, yelling at the top of his lungs as the crowd showed its appreciation. Gardner was declared the winner after the next rider, and Simon leaped to his feet once again.

"I need to get ready," Simon told Jacky, who was sitting next to him. He lightly touched Jacky's shoulder and then left the stands. He went to the truck to get his gear and then strolled to the area reserved for riders. Gardner was still there, putting his things away, and Simon clapped him on the back. “You looked great,” Simon told him.

“Now it’s your turn. I’ll watch your things. Go out there and draw your bull.” Gardner motioned, and Simon hurried out to where the drawing would take place. Then he returned to the area and began getting ready. “What bull did you draw?” Gardner asked.

Simon swallowed and shrugged.

“No freaking way!” Gardner shouted, and the others in the area turned toward them. Gardner had the decency to look sheepish and lowered his voice. “You drew Disorganized Chaos?”

“Yup,” Simon told him and continued getting ready. He’d also drawn a middle ride, so he had some time. The other riders came in, and the chatter increased as they got ready. He half expected Dante to come in to say hello and gab with the other riders, but he didn’t.

Gardner lifted his bag once he was done. “I’ll see you out there,” he said with a grin, and then strode out as though he were on top of the world. Simon spent a few minutes simply being happy for his friend before getting his mind on his ride. He ran through the one ride he’d had on the bull. That single ride that had landed him in the hospital for two days and had made it hard for him to return to his training, no matter what he’d told his parents. And damn if he hadn’t drawn that fucking bull. He’d known he’d have to ride him eventually, so he might as well get it over and done with.

Just before his turn, Simon gathered his things and left the dressing area. Jacky was waiting outside and took Simon’s bag. “I saw the bull you drew,” Jacky said, and Simon nodded slowly. “It’s just a bull like any other.” Simon nodded again. “Go on out there and show them what you’ve got.” Jacky smiled hugely at him, and Simon returned it. The nerves that had been flying through his guts stopped. All was still and quiet in his head as he leaned down and kissed Jacky quickly, after making sure they didn’t have an audience. Then he strode toward the bull chute to wait his turn.

There was one rider ahead of him. He happened to be the current leader. Simon watched as the chute opened. The bull and rider flew out, and, God, if the bull didn't flip the rider right over his head, sending him rolling head over heels along the arena floor. The rider got up and raced to the rails, to the crowd's delight. Today definitely was not a good day for riders.

Simon took a deep breath, released it slowly, and then walked to the chute. He waited while Disorganized Chaos was loaded into the chute. Then he climbed onto the rail and waved to the crowd. He settled on the bull and fixed his grip exactly the way Dante had originally showed him. Then he tested everything and flexed his shoulders before raising his hand and giving the signal.

He and Chaos were off, and the bull tried the same shit he had before. This time Simon was ready, and when Simon didn't fall into the well, the son of a bitch went the other way. Simon decided to change the playbook and spurred the bastard hard. He went straight up and came down with a thud that Simon was ready for. Simon yelled at the top of his lungs, having the time of his life. The bull began spinning again, and Simon held on as his seat began to slip. The buzzer sounded, and he spurred the bull again. It straightened up for a split second, and Simon bailed, rolled onto the sandy arena floor, and then took off for the rail. His heart pounded as he climbed, and he glanced back as the bull was herded out of the arena. Simon waved to the crowd, which was going wild. When he looked down next to the rail, he saw Jacky grinning up at him, holding up Simon's hat. He took it and waved to the crowd.

"Whooee, that ride took guts," the announcer said. "Let's hear it for Simon the Frizz." A cheer went up from the crowd, and Simon waved the hat while pulling off his helmet. Jacky took the helmet, and Simon plopped the hat on his head, then waved to the crowd. The cheering died down and Simon was about to climb off the rail when he heard the cheering continue from one section of the stand. Simon looked over and nearly fell off the rail. He glanced down at Jacky, and damned if the man's grin hadn't gotten bigger.

Simon stood up and waved to the section that was still cheering. He saw his father with Miriam on his shoulders, his mother standing next to him. Malachi and Jeremiah jumped and cheered next to them, as did the rest of the brood from home. They were all there, screaming their lungs out and jumping up and down. Simon waved to them and then climbed down from the rail. "Did you know they were going to be here?" Simon asked Jacky.

"No. They didn't share that with me, but I called yesterday and told them where you were and that you were in contention. It's only a few hours away for them." Jacky grinned and led him around to the arena exit. Simon's score was announced, and another cry went up from the crowd. "I'd say that puts you solidly in first, and one of the other riders is going to need a miracle to catch up."

The day ended up short on miracles, and an hour later, Simon entered the ring, hat in hand, to accept his buckle from the judges. "We understand that you have people here with you today," the announcer said and shoved the microphone in front of him.

"Yes. I have both friends and family here," Simon said, and he waved his hat in their direction, but didn't see them. He heard them before he turned to see them, his entire family standing by the rails, waving, yelling, and jumping up and down. Then he saw Jacky, Dante, and Ryan, along with the other folks from the ranch who'd come to see him ride. This wasn't the world championships. It was just one of the dozens of rodeos held in the west throughout the year, but it felt like he'd won the prize of prizes. Simon thanked the judges and walked over to the group. He climbed the rail, waved one more time to the crowd, and then jumped down onto the other side. He handed his beaming father the buckle and then hugged his mother tight. "I never thought I'd see you at one of these."

She hugged him tighter. "I might never come again, but I had to see you—we had to see you." Simon hugged her one more time and then stepped back. Miriam jumped up and down at his feet, and he picked her up. "Hey, Picklewarts," he said and then hugged his excited baby sister. After greeting all the others, his father took

Miriam and handed him back the buckle. Then Simon moved to where Dante and Ryan stood waiting for him.

"You did us proud," Ryan said and pulled him into a back-slapping hug. He got the same from Dante.

"One hell of a ride," Dante said before letting him go. Then Simon hugged Jacky tightest of all.

"You had me half scared to death," Jacky said, and then everyone gathered around.

"Were you scared?" Malachi asked.

"No," Simon answered him. "Sometimes you have to dare the bull to throw you." He threw his arm around Jacky's shoulders and grinned. Over the past few months, he'd had enough fear and worry to last a lifetime. Now he truly had it all. "Yee hah!" Simon shouted to the sky above, throwing his hat in the air.

ANDREW GREY grew up in western Michigan with a father who loved to tell stories and a mother who loved to read them. Since then he has lived all over the country and traveled throughout the world. He has a master's degree from the University of Wisconsin-Milwaukee and works in information systems for a large corporation. Andrew's hobbies include collecting antiques, gardening, and leaving his dirty dishes anywhere but in the sink (particularly when writing). He considers himself blessed with an accepting family, fantastic friends, and the world's most supportive and loving partner. Andrew currently lives in beautiful historic Carlisle, Pennsylvania.

Visit Andrew's website at http://www.andrewgreybooks.com and blog at http://andrewgreybooks.livejournal.com/.

E-mail him at andrewgrey@comcast.net.

Andrew was the featured author at Two Lips Reviews in Feb. 2010.

The First Ride: A Wild Ride by ANDREW GREY

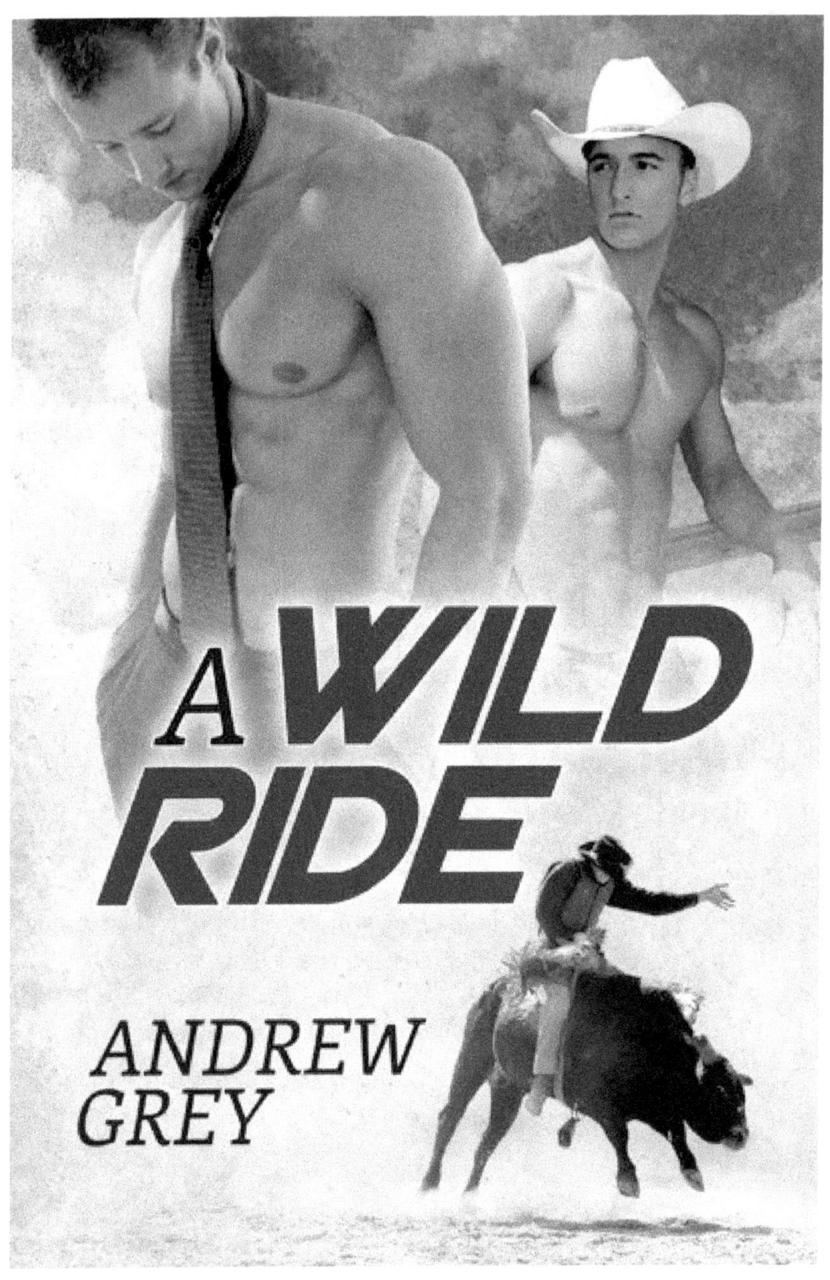

Also from ANDREW GREY

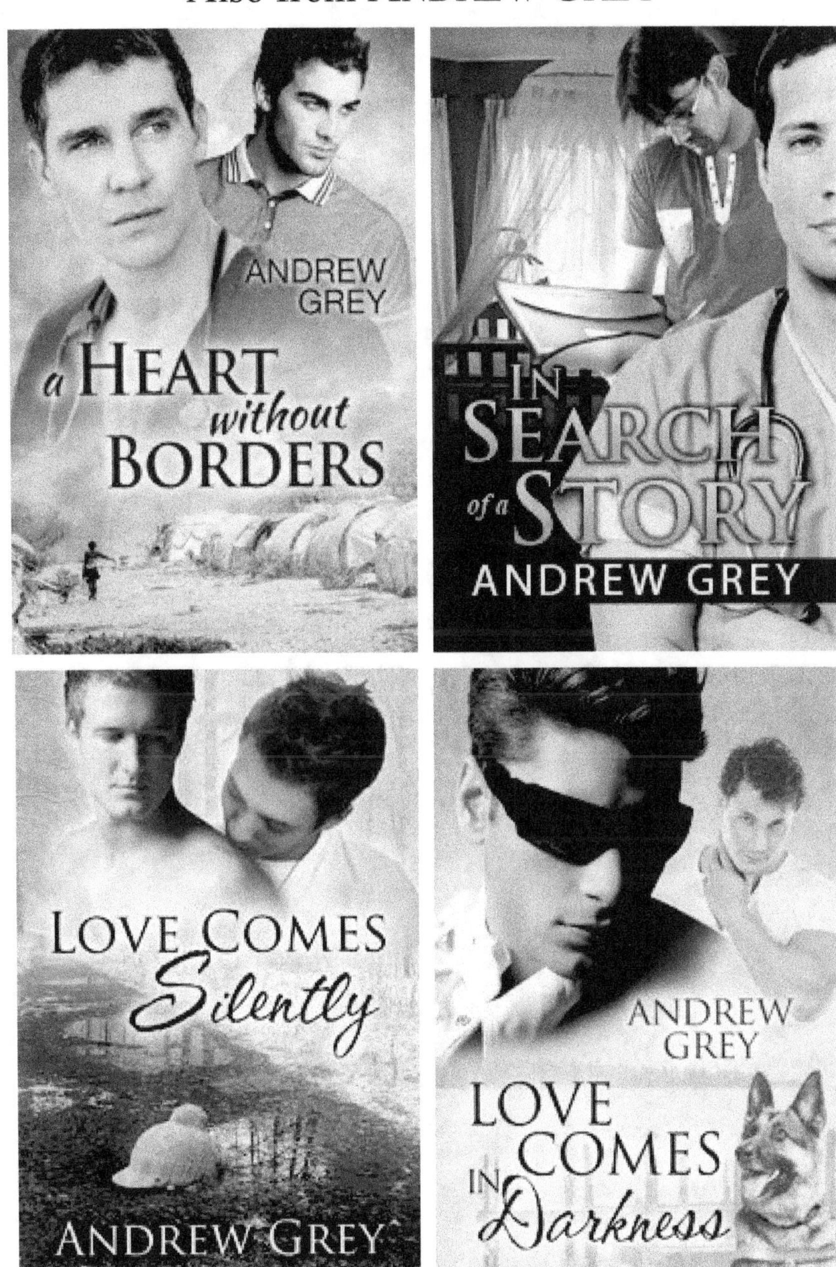


http://www.dreamspinnerpress.com

The Art Series from ANDREW GREY

http://www.dreamspinnerpress.com

The Love Means… Series from ANDREW GREY

http://www.dreamspinnerpress.com

The Love Means… Series from ANDREW GREY

http://www.dreamspinnerpress.com

Fire Series from ANDREW GREY

http://www.dreamspinnerpress.com

www.ingramcontent.com/pod-product-compliance
Lightning Source LLC
Chambersburg PA
CBHW060055260626
47160CB00005B/1682

*9781627980975*